DECOMPOSING MAGGIE

DECOMPOSING MAGGIE

by
Ann Eriksson

TURNSTONE PRESS

Turnstone Press
607-100 Arthur Street
Artspace Building
Winnipeg, MB
R3B 1H3 Canada
www.TurnstonePress.com

Turnstone Press gratefully acknowledges the assistance of The Canada Council for the Arts, the Manitoba Arts Council, the Government of Canada through the Book Publishing Industry Development Program and the Government of Manitoba through the Department of Culture, Heritage and Tourism, Arts Branch, for our publishing activities.

The Canada Council | Le Conseil des Arts
for the Arts | du Canada

MANITOBA
CONSEIL DES arts COUNCIL DU MANITOBA

Canadä

Cover design: Doowah Design
Interior design: Sharon Caseburg
Chapter icons: Lesley Pechter
Author photo: Robert Laing
Printed and bound in Canada by Friesens for Turnstone Press.

National Library of Canada Cataloguing in Publication Data

Eriksson, Ann, 1956-
    Decomposing Maggie / Ann Eriksson.

ISBN 0-88801-283-7
    I. Title.

PS8559.R553D42 2003   C813'.6   C2003-906489-1

Turnstone Press is committed to reducing the consumption of old growth forests in the books we publish. This book is printed on acid-free paper that is 100% ancient forest free.

Dedicated to all my children

Camas ~ the wildflower
Malaika ~ the angel
Noah ~ the island boy
Devin ~ the feeder of eagles

In memory of Georg

Not for me steel coffins
Nor even a pinewood box.
Lay me out in the wilderness
And let me return to Earth.

—Mary de La Valette

DECOMPOSING MAGGIE

Adiantum pedatum
MAIDENHAIR FERN

My husband is dead.

My children are inconsolable. Joy has locked herself in her bedroom, music blaring so loud I can barely hear her sobs. Liam is in the driveway shooting baskets, fast and hard—thud, thud, thud. Do they think they can drown out the roar of the missing heartbeat of the man who lies in front of me? He stares unseeing from beneath half-open eyelids.

These past days, I watched them come to sit with their father. They bubbled over with stories of friends, school, sports—desperate to fill him with life. Or merely to press a morsel of themselves into his withering palm, to take along with him. Dark seeds of sorrow stained their eyes.

I can do nothing for them. I have strength only to stifle my own unbearable grief. And bury the lie I told a dying man.

This morning I climbed into his bed—our last bed. I wrapped my arms around what was left of him. His head

cradled against my breast, I watched his bony chest rise and
fall. His eyes were vacant and I knew he was no longer in
the room with me but in a mysterious, unreachable place.

The only sound was our two breaths meeting in the
space between us.

Our first shared bed was an alpine meadow. The thin,
high air and close sun of a mountainside our blankets. We
were students—he in fine arts, I in teacher's college—in
love and truant from a summer class.

Below us stretched the city of Vancouver; the Lion's
Gate Bridge, the green unsullied sprawl of Stanley Park,
and beyond, the sun glinting off downtown skyscrapers.
Freighters waited before and after the bridge. To the west,
the green and blue of islands and water merged. Above,
bald eagles drifted, wings motionless on the thermal currents of summer.

"Maggie," Peter had asked as he traced pictures of ants
and butterflies along my naked arm with a bit of soft purple
heather, "if you were to do yourself in, you know, commit
suicide, how would you do it?"

I could think of nothing to say. Nor had I ever thought
to put such a question to my own head. Especially on such
a God-given glorious day and I was newly in love.

He rolled onto his back and spread his arms across the
heather. "I think I'd do it like this. I'd lie down on the
ground and . . . and decompose. But not here. In the forest,
under the trees. One day, I'd walk into the forest." He
closed his eyes. "Let's see, an old forest with big trees and
lots of moss. Oh, and near the ocean. It would be nice to
hear the ocean while I'm lying there. I'd walk into the forest and end up a heap of dirt. You wouldn't know me from
the forest floor."

The thought of ants and slugs swarming through his

4

clothes, tunnelling into his perfect skin, his sea-blue eyes gaping holes, was more than I could bear. I must have cried out. He stopped drawing on my arm and stroked my cheek, softly laughing in that way he did, and whispered not to worry.

I did not run madly down the mountainside from the knowledge that early widowhood would not suit me. Or recommend to him he needed psychiatric help. Instead I was awed. This man is not afraid to share his deepest secrets with me. I was to learn that Peter contemplated everything. Nothing escaped his philosopher's heart: the magic of water, the meaning of stars, the sweetness of children. The man who created ants and butterflies on my arm with a bit of heather was a giver of life, not a taker.

"Look, Mags." He had curled back against me, his head on my shoulder. "Think about it. My cheek against yours. Can you tell where I end and you begin? That's what it feels like under me too. I can't tell what's me and what's plant. And if I stay here long enough, me and the plant will turn into another separate thing. Two become one. Incredible."

He pulled me over on top of him, laughing. "Let's see if it works for people."

We made love for the first time that day, the eagles our only witness. Our limbs stained with the fleeting pigments of the meadow—the purple of heather, the gold of arnica, the scarlet of Indian paintbrush. The boundaries between us blurring until I could no longer distinguish his skin from mine.

In the years since that day, I came to know the nuances of Peter's body more intimately than I knew my own. But the past months had transformed him into a stranger, and reduced our landscape to a simple bed in a darkened room.

Our last bed. This morning, there was no warm fragrance

of flowers, no sunlit vista, no butterflies on my arm—only Peter's failing body slumped against my shoulder. When he moaned, I rose to prepare a syringe of morphine to ease his pain. As I squeezed the clear fluid between his blackened lips, I studied his face. The gaunt hollows in his jaundiced cheeks, the sunken eyes, the broken, ragged line of mouth. I struggled against the moment when the atoms of Maggie would be torn from those of Peter. When I would have to learn once again, like a newborn, to breathe on my own, to think my own thoughts, to teach my heart to beat in time only with itself. What did it take for the earth of the forest floor to differentiate into separate beings? For a flower to sprout, a tree to grow, for me to go from being Maggie and Peter to Maggie alone?

I held his hand and watched for the drug to smooth the furrows from his brow. His flesh hung flaccid from his bones, his urine running black into a diaper. He no longer walked the few steps to the bathroom, his feet and legs bruised with pooling blood. My daily massaging had brought little comfort. His hair—there was no hair, no eyebrows, no faint moustache—shed long ago. Already a skeleton.

But there was a fragile calm about him I had not felt before. His eyes opened. Those wise blue eyes, the last recognizable remnant of my husband. His dry, swollen tongue rolled slowly across his lips. He spoke, his voice hoarse and weak. I could not hear. I leaned closer, his tepid breath warm against my cheek.

"Take me to the forest."

I froze. Had he read my thoughts? Were we still, even at this terrible parting, of one mind? My heart lightened a little.

"Take me to the forest."

His thin voice twisted in my conscience. I could have done as he asked. I could have gathered his body, feather light, in my arms, and walked with him, through dry leaves and cool autumn air, along the road to the park at the end of the street. I could have laid him on a bed of moss and maidenhair fern, his head supported by a half-rotten nurse log. He would smile at me and nod, grateful. But would his substance then begin to fade? Would I see through him to the details of the fern fronds below, graceful, dark stems against delicate green leaves? And on the cracked and broken texture of the log, would a tiny wood bug twirl where Peter's shoulder should fall? Would he diminish until the impression of his body in the spongy moss was all that was left? Would he become earth before my eyes?

7

No! How could he ask this of me? I covered my ears and twisted from his pleading, sunken face so stark against the gay print of the pillowcase. He grabbed my arm with startling strength, forcing me to turn to his dying, trusting eyes. He repeated the words with the last remnants of his ebbing tide. *"Take . . . me . . . to the forest."*

Even as I had nodded, I had known it was a lie, that simple gesture of my head. I knew when he next slept, I would release him from his pain. He would cross the imperceptible line between life and death.

And now, as I sit with his body and wait, I know when they come for him in the twilight hours and ask what is to be done, I will not hesitate to answer. *Cremation.* For his ashes, I will weave a basket of kelp adorned with cedar bark. He will smell the fragrance of the trees and the sea and rest with the illusion I have fulfilled his dying wish. But I will not scatter his ashes as we did for our Angel. The three of us in our rowboat, Liam singing about pretty horses and sleeping babies, flinging handfuls of ash and wildflowers gleefully into the sea. I will keep Peter with me always. For without him, I too will die.

Peter had watched me nod, his eyes steady on my face. I wonder now, did he know it was a lie?

ONE

Maggie Cooper knelt on the sunroom floor of her West Vancouver home and sorted through the found treasures of her day. The sharp odour of fresh seaweed and salt spray expanded into the room from the grocery bags at her knees. One by one she pulled items from the tangle in front of her. Shells in one pile: blue mussel, limpet, butter clam, a crab pincer. Seaweeds in another: ropes of bull kelp, rockweed, paper-thin sea lettuce, crinkly Turkish towel. She slid the slippery plants into tubs of salt water. Later she would transfer them to a fresh water bath to wash away sand and salt, before hanging them to dry in the sun; smaller sea-weeds on wooden laundry racks against the wall, and bull kelp tied together in long, loopy circlets and hung from hooks in the ceiling. In a third heap she placed strips of cedar bark and swatches of grey-green lichen, spongy mosses, honeysuckle vine and curiously shaped driftwood. These she arranged on a floor-to-ceiling shelf next to the door. She crushed a handful of cedar needles between her fingers and held them to her nose to banish the rancid smell of the neglected house. This was her favourite part. This moment when the wild materials began to insert themselves into the stale, empty rooms and take over.

She opened the French doors; the air from the back garden mingled with the sea smell. A crow cawed from the maple tree in the next yard. A breeze blew in from the alley and eased around her. When she wasn't out walking the local beaches and forests for materials, Maggie worked in the sunroom. This was her haven, her sanctuary.

Here she could avoid evidence of Peter scattered throughout the house. The painting on the hallway wall—Wilson's warblers on the branch of a salmonberry. She had watched him paint it, witnessed it come to life beneath his hands. Flame-orange berries and yellow wings, the smooth head of the bird, its eye bright, wiry feet gripping branch. She could take it down; she knew that. Put it in the basement and replace it. A Bateman print, a calendar, nothing . . . a blank wall. But she knew the imprint of it would remain, scored onto the lenses of her eyes, permanent.

The living room, his favourite chair. A black leather recliner. He would sit there in the evening, a glass of wine in hand, music—Mozart or Rachmaninoff, Pavarotti, if he was in the right mood—on the stereo. Eyes closed, a contented smile on his face. Maggie sat there on occasion now. When she could bring herself to be in the room alone. Hoping the arms of the chair would become his and hold her.

The front bedroom, the master, where one side of the closet was empty. The children insisted the clothes go the day Joy came home from school and found Maggie making dinner in Peter's one dress shirt and tie. They called Uncle Mark, who came over in his battered, orange VW van. Mark was dark and quiet, small and lithe, younger than Peter. So different from his brother. A social worker for the city, he always knew what to say. Never angry, always kind. He led Maggie to the bedroom and opened the closets. He sat beside her on the flowered bedspread and gently took her hands into his.

"Peter's gone, Maggie," he said.

"I know," she had whispered, not looking at him.

She brought up a box from the basement and packed up Peter's clothes. Everything—socks, boxers, jeans, his t-shirt collection. Mark and the children hauled the heavy box out to the van, then stood helplessly by as she filled a second box with her own clothes. She saved a couple of pairs of jeans, two t-shirts, and an old, grey, paint-spattered sweatshirt of Peter's. Maggie wore the sweatshirt now. She liked the worn softness of it against her skin and the sweet smell of Peter still lingering in its fibres.

Upstairs, at the top of the bum-worn, curved banister, were the children's bedrooms, both empty. Her two children had floated away like wisps of dandelion fluff after the blooming was finished. As if they had nothing left to hold them here, after the father was finished. First Liam to Rose ...then Joy to where? Maggie couldn't remember anymore. She was just gone one day.

More artwork hung in the kitchen: a pen-and-ink illustration of an alligator lizard on a fallen oak leaf, a family portrait at Ambleside Park, a charcoal collage of intertwined bird bones, beaks and feet. It made her whirl sometimes, the assault of memories. Images flashing past: Peter's coffeemaker, his favourite pottery mug, the fridge magnet he gave her that read "Martha Stewart doesn't live here." The unpainted quarter-round at the base of the cupboards, where he had been interrupted. Where pain had bent him double. It was too much. Walking through her house was too much.

But this room of glass was different. Even though it had been built by Peter after their move from the island nine years ago, she didn't feel him here. As if the walls of windows could not hold him.

A wooden work table dominated the room. Shells and half-dried seaweeds, feathers, vines and driftwood littered the surface. A jumble of tools crammed two open drawers: knives of different sizes, scissors, a leather punch, an awl, clippers. Stacks of newsprint, tins of finishing oil, misting bottles and a bucket of clothespins crowded the long under-shelf. A glue gun—its cord dangling—hung from a nail on the wall.

Maggie slipped off her wedding rings, ran water into the utility sink and unhooked a length of dried bull kelp from the ceiling. Although gathered months ago, it still smelled faintly of the sea. Leather-hard and stiff in her arms, the long, withered stipes rattled together as she plunged them into the bath. Within minutes, the water relaxed the stalks into workable coils that settled to the bottom of the sink.

Maggie lifted out the snarled bouquet with both hands, shook the excess water free and threw it onto a plastic sheet on the floor. The beach smell blossomed into the room. A pair of scissors on a string around her neck, she squatted to pull apart the jumble. A number of plants were perfect from holdfast to float and these she eased from the pile and set aside. Out of the remaining assortment, she chose the best lengths, snipping out rotten sections that came apart in her hands. When she had a dozen and a half good pieces, each an arm's length and two fingers wide, she moved them to the table and pulled up a stool. She ran her fingers along each, feeling again for soft spots and imperfections, then returned three to the pile on the floor. She nodded—satisfied.

Maggie wove eight lengths into a flat bottom the size of a dinner plate. The loose ends splayed out across the table like the spokes of a wheel. Twining a double-stranded weaver of thin kelp cord over and above the spokes, she completed the bottom, clipping the strands together with a clothespin. A second thicker weaver became the first layer of the sidewall, pulling the spokes vertical. Another clothespin. Then the second, layer of wall. Her head bent, intent on her work, Maggie was oblivious to the gathering dusk.

Around her, mounded floor to ceiling against every wall, were baskets, dozens of baskets. Crafted from seaweed, adorned by riches from beach and forest. All sizes and shapes; each unique. A basket so petite it held only a single limpet shell, another big enough for a tree. Some lidded, others with handles. They lined the windowsills, flowed across the floor, under the table and out the door into the hallway like an ocean wave surging through the house. They shone soft with the muted colours of dehydration: honey gold and brown-red, the blacky green of dried algae mixed with the dusty white and blue of shells, the orange and pink of the hard creatures, the warm burnish of cedar. Textured by the hand of nature. The warp—kelp stipes and shells from the sea; the weft—the fragile tendrils of her memory.

Clinocardium nuttallii
HEART COCKLE

Today I gazed on paradise. Peter told me we would walk to Kits Beach to paint the fall colours. I should have known better. Peter didn't *just* do anything. There was always a catch, a surprise. This excursion was no exception.

He showed up at my West Tenth basement suite a half hour early, wearing cycling shorts, his bike hanging on the rack at the back of his car.

"Change of plans," he said after his usual exuberant hello kiss. "Put on some riding gear and bring a warm jacket and pants. I'll throw your bike on the car."

"Where are we going?" I followed him barefoot into the crisp air and sunshine of an Indian summer day. His eyes were the same colour as the sky.

"Oh, you'll see," he answered as he wheeled my bike from the garage and hoisted it onto the rack.

"Well, should I at least pack a lunch?" I asked, having experienced other secret day trips with Peter when he expected us to survive on love and anticipation.

"All taken care of." He snapped a bungee cord around the bikes to keep the front wheels from spinning. Grabbing me by the waist, he ignored my half-hearted protests, hoisted me over his shoulder and carried me inside. "Now we only have to get you ready."

As we drove through Vancouver, an aria playing on the cassette deck, I offered names of possible destinations. "Queen Elizabeth Park? Boundary Bay? Steveston water-front?" All prime sketching spots. Peter shook his head at each one until, finally, he began singing along with the tape.

When I was sure we were heading for White Rock, he took the exit to the ferry terminal for Vancouver Island. We drove from bright sunshine into a wall of heavy fog. Peter parked the car on the shoulder of the causeway and unloaded our bikes. A great blue heron stood wraithlike on one leg at the edge of the beach.

"Vancouver Island," I shouted. "We're going to Victoria, aren't we?"

Peter strapped a pannier on the rattrap carrier of his bike, swung his long leg over and pushed off.

"Only the herons know for sure," he said as he disappeared into the fog.

But we didn't go to Vancouver Island. We wheeled our bikes into the belly of the smaller Gulf Island ferry and sat huddled on deck in our rain gear while the boat sailed ghostlike through the grey, soundless world.

"Saltspring? Mayne? Pender? Saturna? Galiano?" I continued my guessing. "This ferry only stops at those five places."

Peter resorted to kissing me to end my quizzing.

Even though I was raised in Vancouver, I had never been to the islands. I often wondered what it would be like to live on a sparsely inhabited fragment of land, cut off from the

16

rest of the world by water, an infrequent boat the only escape.

When we reached the first ferry dock—Galiano Island— Peter stood and offered me his hand. The fog had lifted slightly and we saw clusters of homes and a hotel through the tattered curtain of mist. I shivered at the cold, uninviting scene.

"Peter," I groaned. "Would you please tell me what we are doing here?"

He pulled me to my feet. "Don't worry. You'll like it. I promise."

We cycled off the ferry and through the village of Sturdies Bay. It seemed a ghost town this early on a Sunday; the post office, the one store, even the gas station were closed. I zipped my jacket up around my neck and trailed Peter down the narrow, two-lane road. We followed the edge of a small bay where wooden sailing boats drifted, reflected perfectly in the glassy surface. After a hardware store and a ramshackle community hall, all signs of habitation slowly fell away. A high, green tunnel of trees overhung the unmarked, deserted road.

I soon discarded my jacket and leggings, the hills so steep I resorted to weaving back and forth across the hill face to ease the climb. Peter floated up the inclines, stopping often to wait patiently for me. I fixed the mysterious reward in my mind to distract myself from my burning lungs and legs.

When we finally hit a flat stretch, the noon sun had burned away the fog and patches of light filtered down through the trees. Peter rode hands-free, his arms stretched out to his sides, singing the same aria from the car at the top of his lungs. Watching him, all my annoyance of the morning dropped away and I knew I loved this free-spirited man.

Peter sped ahead and disappeared around a curve. When I rounded the same bend, he had vanished; the road was empty as far as I could see. A dirt road angled off to the left and I caught sight of bicycle tracks in the dust. I free-wheeled down the one-lane track. A forest thick with ferns and blackberry rose on one side and fell away on the other. One steep curve and the hill settled into an open flat ending in a bank of tall firs and cedars. Peter waited, leaning on his bike, arms folded.

"About time," he said, grinning.

I leaned my bike against a tree, then drank from my water bottle. The air smelled of salt; waves splashed on rocks nearby. A trail opened up at the edge of the forest.

"Let's go down to the water," I said.

Before I could take two steps, Peter wrapped a bandanna around my eyes.

"Not so fast there, Mags," he said, "this event calls for a blindfold."

He guided me down the rough trail. I shuffled along gingerly, my hand gripping his arm. The water sounds grew louder and the air cool and moist. At last he let the blindfold drop.

I blinked at the sudden assault of light. We stood on a sandstone shelf at the edge of a half-circle cove. A few houses dotted the shoreline; thick forest bordered horizontal benches and rugged cliffs. Here and there the porous stone had been worn by weather and water into rounded caves. In the middle of the cove was an island, its silhouette like a sleeping porcupine, spikes of trees along its back, fir and the odd twisted red arbutus. A skirt of steep rock joined the forest to the sea and, along the inside shore, pockets of beach sifted gradually into the water. A flock of sea ducks paddled as a black and white unit in the calm behind the island.

"Well, do you like it?" Peter asked.

"It's beautiful," I said. "But what is it?"

"Your future home."

"My future home?" I raised my eyebrows in question, but he only grinned and nodded at the island. I looked for signs of occupancy. There was no dock, no sign of a trail, no shed or building of any kind.

"You're the dreamer, aren't you?" I said.

"No dream. It belongs to my granddad. He bought it after the war. It's promised to me."

"You want to live there?"

"No, I want us to live there. You and me and our children."

My mind spun with his intimation. The topic of living together had not yet come up between us, let alone where. And certainly nothing as far-fetched as a tiny, undeveloped island.

"But what about our careers?" I objected. "I can't teach here, how are you going to . . . your art—"

"We can do anything we want. We'll manage. Only one problem." He frowned. "I thought there would be a boat."

He scrambled down the rocks and along the water's edge. I tagged behind, jumping from rock to rock to log to keep up. My eyes tracked his lanky body across the rough beach. I had come to assume we would, some day, set up house; I couldn't imagine life without Peter. I stopped on a drift-wood bole and surveyed the island again. An otter glided along the shoreline, barely making a ripple in the sheltered water. Its sleek head shone in the sun. Living here was far from my dreams. For an instant, I saw a pair of children, a boy and a girl, standing on one of the pocket beaches. The boy swung a long bull kelp stipe back and forth in front of him, the girl sang as she hopped over the kelp like it was a jump rope. Then they were gone.

"Granddad used to bring a car-topper with him," Peter yelled from the bank of a pebble and sand beach, where an umbrella of enormous maple trees, their roots anchored in the foreshore bank, hung high over his head. "But there was usually a canoe or a dinghy hidden up here." He looked disappointed. "I wanted to take you out there."

I don't know what it was—the forlorn look on Peter's face, the vision of the children, the colours of the autumn leaves against the now cobalt sky—I knew I had to get there too.

"We'll swim," I decided. "If that's the only way to get there, we'll swim."

I kicked off my shoes and socks. Peter jumped down to the beach, his feet crunching on the broken shells and gravel.

"It's cold, you know. Real cold."

"Can't be that bad. Besides, it's not very far." I stood in my shorts and t-shirt, shading the sun from my eyes as I calculated the distance between the islands. "Well, are you coming? This was your surprise, remember?" I waded into the water, fighting a grimace at the stinging cold.

Peter ran a hand over his sandy curls. Then, without hesitation, he unzipped his jacket and stripped off his clothes. We waded cautiously over barnacle-encrusted rocks. Slimy eelgrass curled around our ankles. A shore crab scurried over my toes and I stifled a scream. By the time the icy water was to our waists, my skin prickled with a thousand needles and my breath caught in my throat. I looked over at Peter and we began to giggle, then turned and charged, heedless of the rocks, back to shore where we stood, giddy with laughter and the first stages of hypothermia.

We struggled into dry clothes and sprawled on our stomachs on the sun-warmed sandstone until the shivering stopped. Peter pulled me towards him and blew hot breath down my neck.

"I've never brought anyone here before," he said.

"Never?"

"Nope." He twisted a strand of my hair around his fingers. "I wanted it to be the right person."

Suddenly I felt shy and tongue-tied. The island tugged at me from the middle of the cove. *I want us to live here. You and me and our children.*

"Wait here." Peter shifted and rummaged in his pannier. Then he was gone, bounding across the rocks around the corner to the beach.

I leaned back against the coarse stone. I imagined Peter and I living on a cliff above the sea, in a house of our own, a calendar photo view from every window. We would have to row all our supplies over. Heat with wood. Use an outhouse. Perhaps I could teach at the local school and Peter could paint. The Gulf Islands were rife with artists. I felt myself settle into the idea. We would manage.

Peter startled me out of my musings. He was crouched in front of me, holding out a fat, deeply ribbed shell mottled russet and brown.

"It's the shell of a heart cockle," he said. "Look inside."

He opened my hand and placed the cockleshell in my palm. I ran my thumb over the fan of bumpy, intersecting ribs and then pulled the two hinged shell halves apart. A whiff of mouldering beach life drifted out.

Inside, a cushion of black sea moss held a slender band of gold inset with a single diamond.

"It was my grandmother's." He lifted the ring from the shell and took my hand. "And now it's yours," he said as he slid it on to my finger.

The light in his eyes dazzled me. Behind him, across the narrow channel, the island beckoned. An eagle pair perched side by side on a high fir branch, as if waiting for my response. As I laughed aloud and wrapped my arms around Peter's neck, I thought I glimpsed the children again, wading through the shallows, tossing bits of heaven into buckets.

TWO

Maggie worked late until her fingers ached and her eyes could no longer focus in spite of the bright glow of the reading lamp clamped to the table edge. She took off her glasses and pressed the heels of her hands against her eyelids.

She studied the two new baskets on the drying shelf. The first was a standard weave, the second a coil made from a trio of complete bull kelp plants. She had inflated the stipes, and then stacked the fat ropes on top of one another like a potter would build a pot with a roll of clay. Cord weavers held the bottom and sides secure, the bulbous floats protruding from the coils like stunted appendages. It had a crude, primitive appearance that pleased her.

To hold their shape while drying, she stuffed the two baskets with balls of newsprint. After a week or so of daily turning, the strands of kelp would shrink and harden to the consistency of bark. To preserve the colours and prevent cracking, she would brush on a coat or two of oil. She rotated the woven basket. A lid would be nice. She eyed a desiccated seastar she had been saving for just such a purpose.

She switched off the light and stood in the dark room. The moon hung in the sky behind the apple tree in the garden, as if caught in the bare branches of the canopy. She bent forward and pressed her arms down on the table to stretch out her back muscles. In the kitchen, she rummaged through the fridge. A piece of cheese and a withered apple wasn't much for dinner but it would have to do. She would shop tomorrow.

She carried a glass of water to the bedroom door and hesitated before going in. Every night Maggie stood in the doorway, reluctant to enter. The simply furnished room appeared innocent and welcoming. Her most recent basket sat on the bedside table, the box of Peter's ashes inside. She could carry it easily in her two hands, yet it filled the room with a power that left her breathless. Perhaps another basket, perhaps one of the two on her work table, would keep him more contained.

She pulled on her flannel nightgown and slid under the down quilt. It still felt strange to sleep alone. The empty space beside her was enormous, a chasm of emotion she could not cross. Occasionally she woke in the night to find an arm or leg had fallen across the unseen line down the middle of the bed and she would feel confused for a moment. Why had it not met with warm flesh, the curve of his back solid under her touch, the bristly hair on his legs? When she remembered, when the realization washed over her, she would pull her own limbs back and wrap them around herself. It was never any comfort, though. Her own embrace could not fill the emptiness inside.

The air in the room felt weighted, burdened. She should

24

open the window, but the heaviness of exhaustion bore down on her. She prayed she was tired enough to spend a dreamless night, and wake in the morning refreshed and ready to meet the day.

The dream found her quickly. Maggie shuffled like a blind woman through darkness, hands weaving randomly before her, feeling for Peter. She sought thick curls, soft skin, warm breath. But found only a wall—smooth, hard and cold. A ceiling inches above her head. To the sides, more walls. Her body tightened, her breath laboured. She turned and ran back, stooping, arms outstretched, fingers splayed, only to hit another wall.

She collapsed, sobbing, into drifts of fine dust. She brought a handful to her nose. The dust swirled around her, flooding eyes, nostrils, mouth. She gagged and clawed at her face, then stopped, startled by its odour. The smell of Peter's skin when she buried her face in his neck, the sweat of him at night, his scent in an empty room. She filled both hands, but she could not hold him. He slipped through her fingers like smoke. There was only dust and darkness. She beat her fists against the wall. *Get me out of this place!*

Maggie stumbled onto the front porch and into the dead of night. The dawn had not yet cast its thin glow over the city to the east. Her hands trembled from the dream. Her nightgown was damp with sweat, her feet bare and cold on the worn boards. She ran down the steps and along the unswept path, where patches of moss and weeds sprouted from cracks between dirt-stained bricks. She stood on the boulevard, bewildered, the sickly light of the street lamp casting her shadow back into the neglected yard. Old, dry leaves were plastered against the bottom of the wrought-iron fence and storm-blown branches littered the lawn. The hundred-year-old house, illuminated only by the weak porch lamp, held none of its former charm and warmth. She saw the house as a stranger would, the stained-glass windows spotted and unwashed, the paint on the casements and shingle siding peeling. Even the great blue heron, crafted in glass on the heavy front door, was no longer inviting.

Where to go? To escape this dream that came to her each night and left her empty and frightened, her arms longing, her heart like stone. This dream had turned her home into a prison, doors wide open but from which she could not break free.

She ran up the street and into the middle of Taylor Way. The thoroughfare, thick with noise and the gaseous stink of cars during the day, was deserted. She walked into the four-lane road and stood on the yellow line. She faced downhill toward the sea, then uphill to the mountains. Staggering a few steps north, she then retraced the same steps south. Her head swirling, she held her arms up above her head, shaking them in the cool night air, and screamed an anguished cry to the empty city.

A taxi turned up from Marine Drive, its engine working on the uphill climb. It rushed toward her, the driver's face white, eyes startled behind the windshield. He honked the horn and swerved the car around her to continue up the hill. Maggie watched the tail lights fade and heard the engine roar diminish. When it was a speck of light far up the hill, she ran back down her street.

When she reached the house, she turned into the driveway and stood panting by the station wagon. She felt for the magnetic key box hidden in the wheel well and opened the door. Sliding into the driver's seat, she slammed the door

and felt for the ignition. The key fell from her shaking fingers. She groped around on the gritty floor, the leather
wheel cover pressing into her cheek until her fingers closed
over the cold metal. She turned the key in the ignition and
the engine roared. The transmission squealed as she
jammed the stick shift into reverse. The car lurched and
stalled. She tried again. The engine churned, spluttered and
died.

"Goddamit," Maggie swore. She folded her arms across
the top of the steering wheel, laid her head down and cried.

Hours later she woke slumped across the front seat, the
stick shift digging into her side and the sun high in the sky.

For the rest of the day, Maggie worked in the sunroom. She
stopped for a short break to fix a cup of coffee and a piece
of toast, but she was anxious to use up the drying kelp
before it was too stiff to bend. It was early evening when the
doorbell rang.

Maggie groaned. She hated interruptions. Visits from
friends were rare; she didn't encourage them. When the
bell ringer persisted, she stood at the end of the hallway
where she could see through the stained glass in the front
door. Paula? Tension knotted her stomach at the thought of
her old friend. It had been months, a year, since Paula made
the ferry trip and the drive from Galiano Island to ring the
bell, standing patiently outside, listening for footsteps that
never came. But it couldn't be her. There were two people
at the door. A pair of brown eyes blinked through the clear
glass below the curved neck of the heron. Someone else
pressed the ringer repeatedly, calling her.

"Mom!" It was Liam. "Mom, are you in there?"

Maggie opened the door. Liam and his girlfriend, Rose,

tumbled into the hallway. As a couple they were both comical and striking. Rose, who stood only to Liam's chest, was as dark as Liam was fair, as voluptuous as he was slim. "Hello, we're here," they yelled. Liam stooped and threw his arms around Maggie, his hair smelling of cool night air.

"Liam, what are you doing here?" Maggie said, arms limp at her sides.

28

"Did you forget? It's Friday, our dinner night. I called and left a reminder," he said, pulling a paper bag from his pocket and hanging their coats in the hall closet.

"Dinner?" She had long ago decided to ignore the flashing light on the answering machine in the kitchen. "Oh. I . . . yes, I must have forgotten. I was working."

"Never mind, Mom," Rose said, kissing Maggie's cheek. Rose had insisted on calling Maggie "Mom" since she and Liam moved in together. Maggie had never corrected her. "We came over to see you. Dinner isn't important. I'm sure we can come up with something to eat."

Like a couple of puppies, they carried on down the hallway to the kitchen, holding hands and jostling one another playfully. Liam pulled open the fridge door to reveal the bare shelves and cast a quick sideways glance at Rose.

"Okay," he said. "How about Chinese?"

"I . . . I plan to shop tomorrow," Maggie mumbled, flustered. "Chinese is fine, dear."

While Liam phoned in the order, Rose set three places at the table with bowls and old, darkened chopsticks she found in the back of the kitchen drawer. She talked as she worked, going on in her cheerful way about the desk they found for Liam at a garage sale, the curtains she was sewing for the oval window in their attic apartment in Kitsilano, their plans to paint the walls sun yellow. Maggie sat helplessly at the kitchen table, her thoughts back in her workroom with her baskets.

"Get an order of steamed rice too, Liam," Rose called out. "Did Liam tell you he got accepted for the Children's Festival? We're pretty excited about it. It's one of the biggest clown gigs in town."

"No, no, he didn't." Maggie clasped her hands together on top of the table. "That's nice, Rose."

"My kindergarten kids think it's pretty cool my boyfriend's a clown. He's coming in next week to do a show for them."

Liam put down the phone and flopped into the chair across the table from Maggie. It struck her how grown up he appeared, his sandy hair a bit long but neat, his eyes an intense, consuming blue. He was the type of person who warmed up any room he entered, trailing bits of sunshine after him that dropped on the floor and stuck to the walls. An invisible, happy glow lived around him. She longed for the days when he had curled up in her lap and the heat of that invisible glow would enter her, chasing away the shadows. That time was gone. He was now a man, with a girlfriend, a career, a home of his own. Living his own life.

"Dinner should be here soon," he said. "Well, I hope Rose didn't tell you our news."

"Yes, honey." Maggie managed a smile. "It's nice news. Congratulations."

"Nice, it's bloody fantastic." He jumped up and grabbed Rose, dancing her around the kitchen.

Rose laughed, her round face flushed, dark eyes sparkling. "No, Liam. Not that. I didn't tell her about that. I told her about the Children's Festival."

"In that case, we need a toast before we make the announcement."

He pulled a large bottle of sparkling apple juice—corked

and wired like champagne—from the paper bag. Posing like a maitre d', he shook the bottle. Rose squealed and hid behind the counter. Maggie watched her son's antics with patient confusion.

Her son the clown. She and Peter had always wondered what would become of their Liam. As a child he grabbed every opportunity to act the fool. As soon as he could talk, he invented jokes and sang amusing or embarrassing songs. He was fascinated with little gadgets that made water squirt, or created rude or unusual sounds. By the time he was five, he rode a unicycle, juggled and had two dozen magic tricks under his belt. Everybody loved Liam: his carefree, easygoing manner, his unbounded imagination, the constant glimmer of mischief in his eyes, as if making you laugh was all that mattered.

He popped the cork and apple juice frothed up out the bottle. Frantically, he pulled glasses from the cupboard and filled them; more juice spilled out over the counter. He placed a glass in front of Maggie and hung his arm around Rose's neck, raising his drink in a toast.

"We . . . ," he turned to Rose, "are going to be parents. And you, Madam, a grandmother."

Maggie looked at the grin spread across her son's face. She didn't understand the words he had spoken. Parents? These two people standing in front of her were mere children. Liam, what was he, twenty-one, twenty-two? They couldn't possibly be ready to care for a child. She felt them watching her. Their eyes searched her face, expecting her to speak simple words, to react.

She stood and forced a smile. "I . . . I didn't expect this. I think . . . well, it's wonderful." Her voice faded out. She saw the disappointment in Liam's eyes at her inadequate response. He sighed. Brushing Rose's hair from her face, he

30

kissed her on the mouth. He knelt, pushed up her sweater and nuzzled her navel.

"It's about the size of a pea. Hello, little pea," he said into her belly.

Rose giggled and pulled him to his feet. They stared into one another's eyes and grinned like idiots. The doorbell rang.

"Ah, the dinner." Liam rubbed his stomach and ran from the kitchen.

They didn't speak about the baby during dinner. The topic hung in the air between them like an unfamiliar scent, begging attention. Liam and Rose chattered about work and their apartment. Maggie said little, picking at her food with her chopsticks. Liam plied her with dishes of Singapore noodles and duck in hot garlic sauce.

"Come on, Mom. You're too thin," he said.

She ate a few spoonfuls to allay his concern but most of the food remained awash with soya sauce in the bottom of the bowl.

"I saw Joy last week," Liam said. He watched her over the edge of his dish as he scraped the last of the rice into his mouth.

"Oh," Maggie said, staring at the pool of apple juice on the counter, unable to meet his gaze at the mention of Joy. "How is school going for her?"

Liam rolled his eyes. "You remember, she finished high school at the end of semester in January. Too bad you missed her grad. She won the art award. She's working at a restaurant on Robson Street." Liam paused. "She asked about you."

"Tell her I'm fine, will you?" Maggie said. "Tell her to come and visit."

"I think she'd rather you called," he said.

Rose shot a warning glance at Liam. She set the cracked teapot on the table with a deliberate thud amid the empty foil cartons, food spills and dirty dishes, and said to Maggie, "What have you been doing with your days, Mom?" She lifted the pot again and poured green tea into three mismatched coffee mugs, all missing handles, and pushed one across the table to Maggie.

"I work a lot on my baskets," Maggie said, curling her hands around the warm cup.

Liam interrupted. "You're still making those—"

"Will you show me?" Rose said quickly. "I love your baskets."

"Of course." Maggie stood. Rose tugged on Liam's hand and he followed her to the sunroom.

Maggie switched on the light. Rose and Liam looked around at the stacks of baskets covering every surface. For the third time that night they exchanged glances. Maggie watched this furtive gesture of unspoken communication with annoyance.

"Would you two like to share your little joke?" Maggie said.

Before Liam could speak, Rose bent over and picked up a plaited basket of kelp whip. At mid-section, an interwoven band of sea urchin tests was caught in the weave like orbiting planets.

"Oh, Mom. It's so beautiful. They all are," Rose said. "Where ever did you learn to make them?"

"My friend Paula and I put a few together on the island, just playing around," Maggie said. "Years ago."

"Would you teach me how to make one?" Rose said.

"I don't know," Maggie said. "I suppose I could. I don't have a real technique. I figure it out as I go along."

"Look at this, Liam, it's exquisite." Rose turned the

basket over in her hands and ran her fingers across the tightly woven bottom. "You should have a show, or set up a booth on Granville Island. These would sell like—"

"Oh, no," Maggie took the basket from her. "These aren't for sale."

"What do you need all these baskets for? They're just filling up the house and getting dusty," Liam said.

"You know, Liam, I've told you before," Maggie said. "They're for your father's ashes."

"How many damn baskets does one man's ashes need?" He stared back at her, his voice sharp. "One, Mother, one."

Maggie held up the basket in her hand. One. But which one? Which basket would be the right one? Which one would bring him peace . . . bring her peace?

"We better go, Liam," Rose said. "I'm tired."

"Sure, sweetie," Liam said. He took her hand. "Why don't you come over to our house next Friday, Mom? We'll do Thai. I know you like Thai. You've never seen our apartment. We can go for a walk to Jericho. The early cherry trees are starting to flower. You'd love it."

"I'll think about it," Maggie said.

As they passed through the kitchen and gathered their coats, Rose picked up a bag and called out. "Fortune cookies, we forgot our fortune cookies."

She passed one each to Liam and Maggie and broke hers open. She pulled out a narrow slip of white paper and read. "You will put on weight. Hah!" She puffed out her cheeks and waddled a few steps. "No doubt I'll be a whale in a few months. What's yours say, Liam?"

"Money will come your way soon," he read.

"Here," Rose fished a coin out of her pocket and flipped it at him. They laughed and looked at Maggie.

Maggie broke the hard, golden biscuit apart. Crumbs

scattered into her hand and down onto her shirt. The paper fluttered to the table. When she didn't pick it up, Liam reached over for it.

"You will go on a journey," he read. "Well, two out of three ain't bad." He leaned forward and kissed Maggie on the cheek. "See you next week? I'll call you."

She could hear them talking and laughing outside as they walked down the street to the bus stop. She gathered the dishes and put them in the sink, then wiped up the spilled juice with a dishcloth. After turning off the lights, she went to the door of the bedroom and stood in her usual spot, staring into the dark room. *Rose pregnant . . . a grandchild. She a grandmother.* She recoiled at the memory of her own babies pressed against her breast, suckling so hard it hurt her, seeking nourishment, seeking life, her life. Had she let them down? Did they still need mothering? Had she loved them enough? Love she thought she understood; she had once possessed it in the fullest way. Like Liam and Rose. Love was solid, sure; she could feel it with her hands, see it in another's . . . Peter's eyes, smell it at the opening of a drawer or in a familiar piece of clothing. She never contemplated love. What she did contemplate, on a daily basis, was death. She didn't, couldn't understand death. How it could be there one day, snatching away something precious, without permission, no apologies. How Peter's eyes could be full of love one minute, empty and cold the next. Where does that last breath go, who hears the last heartbeat? Why can't the arms hold her anymore? She looked out and saw grey, looked inwards and saw grey. Grey permeated everything. Not that she was a morbid person. She loved her children, no question. But when it came to love and death, she could not reconcile the two. Love she knew and had lost, death she craved to understand, but couldn't. Death was in this room, it was all around her and she couldn't grasp it. It slipped through her fingers like smoke.

Decisively, she strode across the room and stripped the quilt, a pillow and the bottom sheet from the bed. She carried the bedding and her nightgown outside to the car and threw them into the back seat. After folding the seat flat, she returned to the house. In the basement, she rummaged through the forgotten things that accumulate over years: old skis, strips of gutter, the push lawnmower. She dragged a dishwater-grey, mildewed camping foam outside and spread it out in the back of the car, arranged the bedcovers over it and climbed in, head first, kicking off her shoes in the cavity between the front and back seats. Locking all doors, she stretched out on her back.

The Toyota wagon had always been hers, the last nine years in Vancouver and before, on Galiano. Peter had called it the Toy. Maggie couldn't recall him driving it; he preferred the Land Rover. He claimed he couldn't fit in a toy car. Maggie's toes rested against the back hatch. She fit perfectly. The car felt secure and free from evidence of Peter.

She struggled out of her clothes, into her nightgown, and slid under the quilt. Slowly, heat sifted into her core. It had started to rain. The drumming on the car roof was loud, but soothing. She closed her eyes. The air flowed long and slow from her nostrils. Tension drained from her jaw. Tonight could be the night. The night of dreamless sleep.

THREE

Maggie woke to early morning birdsong, the sun warm on her exposed leg. The sweet scent of spring slid into the car through the partially open window. She pulled her hand from the quilt and traced her finger through the patch of condensation blocking her view of the three Indian plums along the driveway. The first spring shrubs to bloom, their strings of tiny white flowers had withered weeks ago. The Indian plums had been Peter's; he would only plant native shrubs. The French lilac tucked in behind them was her small victory, its dark purple umbels fat with buds. Soon the air would be heady with their rich perfume.

She breathed deeply and stretched out, arching her spine to release the stiffness another night on a foam pad in the back of a station wagon had brought. She gave thanks for another uneventful sleep.

It was three weeks since her first night in the car. It had become a routine. After a few days she discarded the pretense this was a temporary move, like camping out in the backyard during the heat of summer, and quit bringing the bedding into the house each morning. She sewed a curtain for the back window to block the view from the street. The other windows remained uncovered. She liked the morning sun streaming through the windows, and at night, if she curled up close to the door, she could see sky and stars. Two plastic bags filled with underwear, socks and an extra sweater hung over the front headrests. A cardboard box at her feet held a water bottle, a plastic package of oatcakes, her glasses and a book. Her jeans and sweater were folded in the front seat.

She had abandoned her nightgown to the house, sleeping naked, enjoying the freedom of it. She continued to wake several times in the night, disoriented. But she didn't dream, or at least she did not remember her dreams. She didn't wake choking and clawing at her eyes, crying and gasping that she had to get out. She imagined her dreams flew from the car, up through the partially opened window, seeking normalcy in dreaming places—a proper bed, a well-decorated bedroom. It could be she had simply left them inside the house, floating loosely through the hallways, looking for her. But each morning she woke relieved to have been spared another tortured night.

She settled back on her pillow and watched rainbow fragments from a crystal dangling from the front mirror play across the quilt. Above her head, a collage adorned the ceiling: magazine cut-outs of birds and flowers, a photograph of Liam and Joy building sandcastles, a star chart. She liked to linger like this after waking, before dressing and slipping into the house for breakfast. It was peaceful and immediate. No traffic noises, no refrigerator hum, no clock ticking. She didn't occupy her thoughts with the activity of the day; the ghosts were kept at bay.

She started at the sound of footsteps on the driveway. Burrowing into her quilt, she watched a shadow pass along the fogged side window and stop at the driver's door. Maggie glanced at the locks; all four doors were secure. She rolled over and groped on the floor between the seats for a shoe. She eyed the driver's door, ready.

Two spectacled eyes and a large red nose pushed through the crack at the top of the window. Maggie screamed and jumped.

"Liam! What the hell are you doing? Trying to scare me to death?" She threw the shoe at him.

"Hi, Mom." Liam unlocked the door and peered inside, grinning. He scanned the rumpled covers, her dishevelled appearance, the fogged-up windows. "May I ask what you are doing sleeping in the car?"

"That is exactly what I'm doing," Maggie snapped, "sleeping in my car. Who told you I was here?"

He tilted his head toward the next-door house. "Joan Simpson." He dangled a key between his fingers. "She phoned me. Good thing I kept my key."

Maggie reached around the driver's seat and pushed him away. "Nosy busybody." She yanked the door closed and locked it. "It is nobody's business where I sleep."

"Well, I have to disagree," he said, unlocking the door again. "I'm not a nobody."

He slipped into the seat and started the car.

"What are you doing?" Maggie yelled.

"Taking you to breakfast." He peered into the rear-view mirror. "Oh, and would you open that curtain back there, please? It's pretty hard to see out." He backed the car onto the road. "Here, you might want to get dressed." He threw her clothes into the back seat. "I know it's spring, but you'll catch pneumonia in that getup."

"Liam Cooper, stop this car now," Maggie demanded, sitting up, the quilt clutched to her bare chest. "I am not going anywhere but home."

Liam turned on the radio and continued driving, whistling along with the music. Maggie flopped back down on the bed. "I should take you over my knee."

"That would be a first," he grinned. "Besides, you don't look like you are in an opportune position for spanking anyone."

Maggie put her hands over her face and cursed, then reached for her sweater and jeans.

The road under the Granville Street Bridge was clogged with cyclists, pedestrians and vehicles bound for Granville Island. Liam manoeuvred Maggie's car into a narrow laneway and parked against the wall of an ageing brick building. He steered Maggie by the elbow through the crowded cobblestone streets, past an artists' collective, a sailmaker's shop, a brewery and a kayak store, to the Public Market. He pushed open the heavy glass doors into the airy converted warehouse. Inside, the din was overwhelming. Hundreds of voices—vendors hawking to passing customers, the clank of machinery, the lilt of a busker's flute. She grabbed Liam's hand as they threaded through the jumble of stalls crowding the enormous building. Pyramids of apples and grapes, open baskets of potatoes and carrots, and pots of flowers spilled into the corridors. The air was heavy with the sweet smell of chocolate, the rank odour of fish and other seafood, and the fragrance of fresh bread.

She was amazed at the number of people who yelled a greeting to Liam. He must be taller than Peter, more legs than torso. His shoulders were broader under his windbreaker. In his face she read a new expression. What was it? Maturity, stress, could they be the same thing? He was no longer a boy. Dimpled, round cheeks had sharpened to the hard angles of adulthood. Faint wrinkles of responsibility ran across his forehead. When had this happened? When did he crawl off her lap and out into the world? He had always been sweet and even-tempered. No terrible twos, no teen rebellion. Sweetness . . . sweetness all the damn time. Maggie could never refuse him. Like now. Why was she here with him, instead of in her car, hiding from all this busy, noisy, smelly living?

41

Liam bought Vietnamese spring rolls with peanut sauce, and wooden skewers filled with chunks of strawberries, melons and grapes. Maggie followed him outside, carrying two steaming mugs of coffee to the wide, wooden benches at the edge of the wharf. An old man played an accordion in the middle of a flock of pigeons, his hat upturned on the scarred decking. A couple of dollar coins glinted, hopeful, in the bottom of the hat. He smiled and nodded at Liam. A young child—a year, maybe older—ran at the pigeons, arms out, laughing. The pigeons flew up around the accordion player and the gleeful child. People smiled as they passed by. The girl reminded Maggie of Joy. The way she ran headlong into whatever was in front of her, singing, her coppery hair flying in a tangle behind her, chocolate eyes flashing. Joy threw her whole body into life, arms flailing, kicking out in all directions, just to see what would happen. How different her children were. It amazed her to think they had been created from the same source. The thought of Joy perturbed her. She never saw her these days. That must be all it was.

While they ate, Maggie watched the miniature harbour ferries transport passengers across False Creek to downtown and up to the old Expo site. They manoeuvred like water bugs on a pond among the expensive sailing yachts and working boats that motored under the bridge and into Georgia Strait. Cawing seagulls skulked for a meal from any convenient source. She and Peter had come here often as young lovers. There hadn't been any little insect ferries then, and most of the buildings were used for dockyard functions, but the market was the same. Peter loved it here. He said it inspired his artist's soul. They wandered through the stalls, holding hands, sampling delicacies and filling their knapsacks with groceries. They always ended up on the wharf at sunset, kissing and whispering lover's talk until dark.

"Mom." Maggie started at the touch of Liam's hand on her arm. "I didn't bring you here just for breakfast, although I'm sure you could use a frivolous outing."

"Oh, really," she said.

He winked. "I don't imagine the car can be too comfortable." He picked up her hand and unfolded her clenched fingers. "I want to talk to you."

Maggie stared at their fingers—hers wrinkled and dry, Liam's smooth and supple—entwined against her blue denim jeans. A faint tracing of white makeup lined Liam's fingernails. His hands were larger and stronger than his father's. The thought of Peter's hands brought an ache to her chest. They had been her favourite part of his body. She had loved to hold them, to stroke the elegant fingers, to watch them create with paints and brushes, pen and ink. Magic fingers.

"Mom, I'm concerned about you." Liam bent down and twisted his head up so she couldn't avoid him. His blue eyes had darkened, like storm clouds in a summer sky. It had always surprised her, this hint of darkness in her son.

"What could possibly be concerning you? I'm perfectly fine," she said.

"Right, sleeping in your car is fine. I've been standing on my head for hours every day since Joan Simpson called. Trying to figure out what to do."

"I told you that was none of your business."

"Please, Mom, don't try to pretend nothing's wrong. Joy and I miss Dad too. You're not the only one who's sad. But isn't it time to get over it?"

Maggie crossed her arms and stared at the thick planking at her feet. "You expect too much. It's barely been a year and a half."

Liam paused. He rubbed his fingers across his forehead. When he spoke his voice was gentle. "Mom, it's been three years."

Maggie raised her head sharply. "It can't be that long. It was a year in November. Seventeen months now."

"See, you don't even know what year it is. How could it be only a year? Look at Joy and me. I was twenty. Joy was fifteen. Now I'm twenty-three. Three years, Mom," he said. "Three years and five months."

Heat rose within her chest. Where did three years go? She dug her fingers into her palms; the pain steadied her. "I'm fine, Liam."

"Mom, I feel like we've lost you, like you've been swallowed up by a whale and I can't get to you. When Rose and I were over a few weeks ago, I hugged you and felt like my arms went right through you, like you were invisible. It scares me."

The note of panic in his voice reminded Maggie of Liam as a two-year-old. Running through the island house, desperately searching for her in every room, crying "Mama! Mama!" until he found her on the deck watering plants, cutting kindling out back, or up in his room making his bed. He would collapse into her arms, sobbing. "Me lost you, Mama, Liam lost you."

"Mom, are you listening to me? I need you to listen to me. You never go out, your friends have given up trying to see you. When was the last time you saw Joy? You haven't taught since Dad got sick. Do you even have any insurance money left? All you do is make those baskets, all those damn baskets. Now this sleeping in your car. I half expect to find you sleeping in a dumpster on East Hastings next."

Maggie concentrated on an adult seagull sitting on the railing of the wharf. Its white feathers gleamed in the sun. The yellow beak opened and closed as it squawked at no one in particular.

"When is this going to stop?" Liam continued. "I'm not telling you to forget about Dad, but get him down off the altar. Sure he was a great guy. We all adored him. But he was a regular person. Remember all the times he left us alone on the island when he was teaching in Vancouver? And I didn't always like the way he talked to you—"

"Stop!" Maggie ordered. "Don't speak of your father like that."

They sat for several minutes, the silence a vacuum.

At last, Liam broke the impasse. "I'm sorry, Mom. I . . . I just want you back."

She said nothing. She didn't dare. She knew the grey she had been concealing was creeping across her face and down her neck. She stretched out her fingers against her jeans. Yes, a wash of grey was flowing unbidden to each fingertip. She felt transparent. Liam has seen her grief. Why not, she realized with surprise, he was her son. When he was young, when they were together every day, they would often start talking about the same thing at the same time, as if they could read each other's minds. Or was it only Liam reading her mind?

"There's another thing." He paused. "Rose and I decided to get married after school's out, in July. Mom, we want you to help and . . . we need a grandmother for our baby. We need you."

She stared at him. *Grandmother? Yes, the baby.*

"You don't have to say anything now. I know this is a surprise and a lot to take in. But we have to talk about something else. Dan Collier called. There's an offer on the island. They want to take possession by the middle of May. You could—"

Maggie stared across the harbour at the downtown highrises. "I told you to go ahead and look after all that. To leave me out of it."

He took a deep, shaky breath. Maggie reached out, to place her fingers on his lips, to stop him. But it was too late, the sentences spilled out, words tumbled from him. "Rose and I have been talking. We want you to take Dad's ashes back to the island. It might help. It might help you get over things. Besides, isn't it what he would have wanted? You can't carry his ashes around forever."

"No!" She felt like shaking him. "I won't."

"I didn't want to throw this in on top of everything else, but it may make a difference to your decision."

"Liam, didn't you hear me? I said no."

"Let me finish. You can go over, make sure everything is in order and scatter Dad's ashes. It may be the only opportunity. The renters will be out by the end of the month; you can go over the first part of May."

Liam reached up and touched her on the cheek. "Here," he said. From behind her ear he materialized an ordinary, brass house key, attached by a silver chain to a bright yellow foam float stamped with the words "The Marina, Galiano Island."

Maggie stared at the familiar key. "I don't want it. I . . . I can't." She pushed his hand away.

45

"Please, Mom, for Joy and me." Liam dropped the key into the pocket of her sweater. "Go home and think about it for a few days. I would come and help but I have the Children's Festival." He paused. "Mom." His tone pulled Maggie's eyes once again to his. "If not this, please do something."

46

Liam walked Maggie through the crowded streets to her car. Maggie could hear only the thrum of her own heart, as if she were in the middle of a silent movie. Three teenage girls, in tight, flared pants, navels in full view, walked past, their platform shoes soundless on the cobblestones. A one-man band sat at a corner, harmonica at his lips, and flailed noiselessly at drums and cymbals, nodding his head in time with the rhythm. Maggie grabbed for the sleeve of Liam's jacket; the crowd pressed against her. She wanted to tell him to stop, but the words would not form in her mouth. They were at the car. He opened the door, smiled and brushed his lips across her forehead.

"Love you," he whispered.

He turned, waved and was gone, back into the milling crowd. She watched him, her arm outstretched, reaching to pull him back, until he disappeared.

Maggie raged as she drove across the bridge, and through the West End and Stanley Park to the North Shore. How could he! Telling her what to do, making insinuations about how she's handling things, criticizing her for keeping Peter's ashes. Maggie's fingers clenched the steering wheel, the pink flesh turning white with the effort. Maybe she wanted to be sad. She repeated the thought aloud. "Maybe . . . I want . . . to be sad." She felt the shame of each childish word.

The tears started; the road blurred in front of her. She reached into her pocket, searching for a tissue, and touched the soft plastic of the key float.

Lonicera ciliosa
ORANGE HONEYSUCKLE

I have found the place where I wish to grow old. This island of rocks and trees has captured me. I am cradled by the sea on all sides, wrapped in a symphony of wind and lapping water, the melody composed by an ethereal musical genius. In all directions, my eyes are refreshed by the light, and the uncountable shades of green. The air feeds me with a million smells: the tender scent of wildflowers, the sharp tang of salt on the sea breeze, the heavy aroma of rotting humus and warm foliage.

There is no lack of good company. Along the ocean's edge a mink scurries across the rocks and disappears between the sandstone boulders. It must have a den tucked above the high tide line, littered with gritty scat and remnants of crab. Yesterday, a mask-faced raccoon observed me through the living room window from the top of a swaying fir. I see birds everywhere. Dark-headed juncos feed along the ground and through the twisted branches of the oaks. Woodpeckers—white-rumped flickers and red-crested pileated—wake me in the morning with their staccato search for insect breakfast. A cormorant, its wings stretched out to dry on a half-submerged deadhead, floats by with the current. There is an eagle's nest; I can see it from the bedroom window if I twist my head the right way. The eagles sit together, side by side, or one above another, on the tallest branches of the snag beside the house; their white droppings have already coated the new cedar roof shakes. A christening, a dubious acceptance.

I love this place in the way I will love my children, without judgement. It exists, therefore I love.

I can imagine Peter and me, years from now, rocking on the deck, our wrinkled old hands woven together on the arm of one of the chairs, our white hair stirring in the fresh sea breeze, a plaid wool blanket thrown across our knees. We will know everything around us. The age of the orange honeysuckle climbing up the deck post; it sprouted last year about the time we finished building. The number of eagle chicks and how many survived the first winter. The way the rocks on the cliff below us have shifted their position, breaking off and crashing into the sea to become a reef where rockfish feed and seastars cling. What the wind means when it blows from the south. The names of all the trees—Garry oak, Douglas-fir, arbutus; of each wildflower—Indian paintbrush, chocolate lily, sea blush; each shrub—flowering red currant, ocean spray, salal. We will know every creature that shares this few hectares of stone and trees.

The old islanders on Galiano shake their heads. "Wha'dya wanna live out there for. Useless. Can't grow a thing on that pile of rock."

Who needs to grow a thing? It's all here, perfect.

I guess we would have repaired parts of the house by the

time we are old enough to sit on the deck all day, but now it smells of freshly cut lumber. We didn't fell a single tree to make space for it. Three huge Douglas-firs climb through the decks that wrap around the six-sided glass living room as if anchoring the house to the cliffside against the winter winds. One of my favourite spots is the bed, built into an alcove, high and airy, windows to the side and foot. Each morning, when we wake, we are not sure if we are inside or outside.

49

To the southwest, I can see the low rise of Saltspring Island and behind it the blue-grey hills and ragged line of mountains on Vancouver Island. When we are old, Peter and I will notice the minute changes from day to day that span one season to the next. We will know at which dip in the horizon the sun will set today, and every day; which birds arrive on which spring day—the warblers on the first Tuesday in June, the hummingbirds just past March. We'll plan a party for the day the eagles arrive back home from their summer of salmon fishing, and invite the returning grebes and the buffleheads. And we'll dance with our children and they will know too why we baked a cake on this auspicious day.

Yes . . . children. It has been two months since I last bled. I haven't told Peter yet, but tonight, when we sit in front of the fire after a day building garden beds with soil hauled over in the rowboat, I will tell him. Shall I make him guess my secret? I'll whisper in his ear that we have planted something wonderful. Will he read it from the subtle changes in my body, the shape of my face, the texture of my hair? Will he laugh and tell me he already knows? "How could I not," he will say. "Everyone is talking about it. I heard it from the eagle chatter on the afternoon breeze and the alligator lizard down in the garden."

We will drink a toast of blackberry wine and waltz through the arbutus grove. We will celebrate with a swim in the startling cold of the cove, and share our news with the otters, the shore crabs and the heron.

FOUR

Maggie drove up Taylor Way past her street and onto the Upper Levels Highway to the Cypress Bowl Provincial Park turnoff. The narrow park road switchbacked steeply through forest, with occasional open views south to the maze of Vancouver waterways: False Creek, Indian Arm, Burrard Inlet, the Fraser River. Parking at the cross-country ski trailhead, she picked her way through the remnant patches of snow along the trail, mud gathering on the bottom of her shoes. Maggie tucked her hands into her sleeves, the cold persisting in spite of the exertion of the climb. Her breath came out in opaque puffs.

Abruptly, the alpine fir and mountain hemlock gave way to a pocket of meadow, the vegetation devoid of the vibrant colour of alpine wildflowers that would clothe the slopes in a few weeks. She climbed up from the trail to an outcropping of rocks and sat down.

She and Peter had come to these mountains during their courting days to sit and talk, or hike the three-peaked Lions to the northwest. Every winter after the move from the island, they brought Liam and Joy to the park to downhill ski at the Bowl, or cross-country along these trails. In the summer and until snow fell in early fall they hiked here every weekend. The day was clear and she could see to Mt. Baker in Washington and over to the islands. The ferry navigating between Vancouver Island and Tsawassen was a gleaming white marker in Active Pass, Galiano Island to the north. Her eyes followed the backbone of Galiano to the rise behind which she knew their island sat, tucked into the cove on the southwest shore. She had thought they would live there forever. When they moved to Vancouver to send Liam and Joy to high school, they had always intended to go back.

Then Peter got sick. Vague back pains, unexplained weight loss, jaundice. On a stifling hot afternoon in late August, she held Peter's hand as they sat in the opulent office of a respected North Vancouver oncologist. The doctor, his face a blank sheet, threw words at them as he flipped through pages on a clipboard: *cancer, inoperable, metastasis, a few months, no treatment, no hope.* And, as he opened the door for them to leave, *be strong for your children.* They clung to one another in the elevator, stunned. "What's important is to make sure you and the kids are all right," Peter had said. She collapsed against him at his selfless words, as though it was she who had received the death sentence. A desperate round of chemotherapy failed to slow the disease's progress. In spite of herbal remedies, cleansing teas and an unwavering spirit, Peter's body deteriorated rapidly and he died in her arms on a dreary November afternoon.

Maggie shoved her hands into her sweater pockets; the spring sun was too weak for warmth. She'd never go back to the island. Not without Peter. The island was like a past life, a story in a book, a distant memory of a happier time.

What had Liam meant? Peter a regular person. It was so untrue. He was one of a kind. The children had adored him, taken their bearings from him. They were the needles on the compass seeking magnetic north, their father. She had resented, sometimes, how they migrated to him. But it wasn't anybody's fault; Peter didn't make them turn from her to him when he walked into the house. He was charismatic, that's all.

She had always felt she stood safe in Peter's shadow. They had their moments, their petty arguments. But nothing big. Standing, she brushed her hands across the seat of her jeans and walked down to the trail. Liam should be ashamed of himself. Peter was beyond reproach.

Cancer productus
RED ROCK CRAB

Life through the lens of a camera. I like it. Perhaps when my children are grown I will take up photography as a profession. I might specialize in nature photography. Record endangered species before they disappear. My photos might appear on calendars for Greenpeace. Save the sharptail snake, preserve the killer whale. Or maybe I'll do portraits, capture people in their private moments, snatch pieces from their lives. The Maasai in Africa believe you steal their soul when you take a picture. I could be a soul collector.

Today, I'm the resident recorder of the First Annual Solstice Crab Feast. My hands were dripping with garlic butter and crab juice when Peter plunked the camera bag in my lap and said, "Get some pictures of this thing, okay?" Then he ran off to help Mark pull up the canoe. This thing, the Crab Feast, was Peter's idea. Only Peter would think up an event like this. He is the creative one in the family. I'm the stage crew.

So here I sit, on a sandstone boulder at the end of the

two-fingered point, looking through the 70-200 lens of our Contax 35 mm camera, recording history. I feel important, powerful. I can depict this day in any way I want. Wide angle. Macro. I can use the polarizing filter. I can pull people in close-up, illuminate the intimate details of their lives, or emphasize the big picture in a landscape view. Not record history, make it.

56

In the middle of the cove, Paula and Lester are wading through eelgrass beds and bottom sludge like a pair of great blue herons, stalking the elusive *Cancer productus*. Paula has a net, Lester is holding a sawed-off fishing rod in front of him, a noose rigged to the end. They must have a crab on the run because they are both leaping through the water, howling like madmen, in their bathing suits and floppy hats, rubber boots full of water. I don't know how Lester manages to look like he is going out to feed the chickens even in his bathing suit. Paula could wear nothing but overalls and look gorgeous. If I could snap the shutter now, the scene would appear a futile hunt, or I could wait until they hold up the catch—a big male red rock crab, legal size and fighting mad—its sharp pincers raised and open in self-defense. Prizewinners. Ta da. The same scene, the same people, two completely different conclusions, two sets of emotions. Maybe I'll zoom in and write the story of their marriage: the look that flashes between them every once in a while, the way Lester pushes Paula's hair back from her shoulders, the matching grins on their faces as they fling handfuls of water at each other, laughing like hyenas.

They can't stay out there much longer. The seawater is up to their waists. They must be part polar bear. The rest of us took advantage of the noon tide—the lowest tide of the year—minus point two. We waded through ankle-deep water, easily spotting crabs as they scuttled sideways between eelgrass patches. We must have been a sight, twelve of us skulking half naked through the shallows like a colony of herons armed with all manner of crab-catching paraphernalia: nets, paddles, buckets, boathooks. Peter dragged the canoe around on a line so we could throw our catch into a tub in the bottom. I wish I had gotten a picture of us out there. I missed one of Peter at the beginning of the debauchery, standing in the canoe like an underdressed Captain Cook, a paddle upright in front of him, his hat tipped over one eye, as he delivered the rules. A limit of two crabs each, males only, legal size measured across the carapace checked with a ruler, method of capture optional. He made us all swear we wouldn't take another crab from the cove for the rest of the year. Our penance for our day of abandon. It was forbidden to tell anyone else we were catching crabs without a regulation trap—especially anyone with connections to the Fisheries Officer. We wouldn't want to be in jail for the Second Annual Solstice Crab Feast.

Yesterday, I had doubts the First Annual would be a reality. It rained all day, the cove white with breaking waves. I was ready to phone everyone and cancel, but Peter knew it would be fine. I wonder if he has a direct line to God himself. We woke to a flawless day. No wind, no clouds, the channel like glass, June in its intermittent glory.

If I shift a quarter turn to the right, I can frame the evidence of the Crab Feast with the wide-angle lens. Four families clustered on the flat sandstone bench around two Coleman stoves. Steam rises from soup pots filled with crab parts and two fingers of salt water. People are in various stages of preparation and feeding, like a tribe of barbarians caught up in a ritual ceremony. Mark and his new wife, Deliah, interrupted their honeymoon to be here. Mark is pulling a hot crab leg from the pot with a pair of tongs. Deliah is stuffing thick white meat into her mouth. She used a carpenter's hammer to crack the tough red-speckled shell; lemon garlic butter is dripping down her chin and she is laughing. Those two have spent most of the day cuddled inside a cave on the far side of the reef.

Sixteen-year-old Matthew Hollis is pulling a cold-misted bottle of white wine from the water. Matthew looks hopeful, a wine glass in his hand. Hopeful his parents are too busy to notice or too happy to care.

Reuben Hollis has taken it upon himself to be the chief butcher. He says he learned the method from his grandfather. He flips the crab on its back and crushes the underbelly in a single blow with a flat rock. "Kills 'em instantly," he says. He pulls off the carapace and with it the guts and tosses them into the ocean. After a swish in the salt chuck, the claws and small legs end up in the steaming pot. I have to admit the meat tastes fresher than whole-boiled crab. I'll have to try his method later, after I finish making history.

Now the babies. I shouldn't call them babies anymore; they are already two. Liam and Sarah. Paula says they must have been siblings or maybe lovers in a past life. She believes in all that stuff. I'm not so sure, but I do know they are sweet together, splashing around in tide pools with their green mesh goldfish nets, their rubber ducky boots and their mouths covered in sand from eating seaweed. They look like a couple of beach balls in their orange and yellow life jackets.

Earlier, Liam scared me to death. He and Sarah were looking under rocks on the south side of the point where the shelf drops off into eight or ten metres of water. Peter and I were busy lighting the stoves, half watching them. We heard the splash at the same time. I looked up to see Liam in the water, swimming dog-paddle away from the point. His life jacket was abandoned on the edge of a tide pool, the tie dangling in the water. Sarah stood watching him, twirling her hair with one hand, the fingers of her other shoved into her mouth. My first thought was, where did Liam learn to dog-paddle? I was disoriented at the sight of my child swimming away from me. I stood there, not moving, trying to take in the picture.

Peter reacted first. He sprawled on the barnacle-coated sandstone at the water's edge and stretched his arm out to grab Liam's foot. His boot came free in Peter's hand. Liam swam on toward Saltspring. Then I was in the water. I don't remember running across the rocks; I didn't notice the cold. I took two strokes; he hadn't gone far. All the time I imagined him sinking into the green gloom of the sea, his limp body falling slowly out of sight, tendrils of white-blond hair suspended like fronds of seaweed in shafts of watery light. I was strangled by the vision.

But he didn't sink; he paddled along as if he had been swimming for years, away from shore, away from us. I wrapped my fingers, already turning white with cold, around his ankle and pulled him toward me. His head submerged. He came up sputtering. I crooked my arms around his waist and kicked us to shore, handing him up to his father. Mark threw a towel over Liam. I climbed out onto the rock, chest heaving.

Liam held out his arms to me and Peter swung him down into my lap. I hugged him close. Unlike me, he wasn't shivering. He put both hands on my cheeks and pulled my head around to look into my face. His eyes shone.

"Me swimmed, Mama." And then, "Why you put all dat salt in na water?"

Peter crouched down and ruffled Liam's hair with the

towel. He draped another over my shoulders and tucked it around Liam. Peter's chest and knees were scraped and bleeding from the barnacles.

"Here, let me clean that up," I said and dabbed at the drops of blood with the towel.

Peter pushed my hand away and stood up. "I thought you were watching him, Mags," he said.

I frowned, puzzled by his implication. "But with all these people around—"

"Never mind." He paused. "Good save, though," he said and went to light the stoves.

I was rehearsing explanations for Peter in my head when Paula sat beside me with Sarah. Both children nuzzled in to nurse. Comfort food. Paula and I dissected the last few minutes. Did Liam fall or jump? Neither he nor Sarah would tell us. And his life jacket? "It felled off, Mama."

Katie Hollis is watching them for the rest of the day. I told her I would buy her a book next time I was in Victoria if she promised not to take her eyes off those two precious little ones. She's a bookworm. Whenever I see her at the market selling jams and jellies with her mom, she has her nose in a novel. Liam likes Katie. We've had her over to babysit a couple of times. She's responsible for twelve. The kids on the island seem to grow up fast. It must be the freedom. Yes, that will make a nice picture, the three of them peering into the tide pool. Which one will be the first to stick their finger into sticky anemone tentacles and scream? A stranger looking at this picture a few weeks from now will never know how much of a treasure this picture is. For me, it will always trigger a vision of Liam vanishing into a blue-green abyss.

I could leave out all the people. Turn my camera toward Saltspring and shoot the molten light of the afternoon sun

across water. The sailboats motoring up the windless channel, the shiny wet head of a seal as it breaks the surface
without a ripple. Or I will photograph details of the island.
The caves pocketing the shoreline, their contours like
human skin folding upon itself. The weight of the trees at
the top of the cliff straining toward the sea; the transition
of plant to earth to rock to sand to water. I might put on the
macro lens and focus inward. The space between the grains
of sand, the bits of detritus captured on a single tentacle of
a single anemone, the swirl of my own fingerprint.

61

It's a pity photographic emulsion cannot absorb the
sound of gulls crying overhead, laughter of friends, the slap
of waves against land. Wouldn't it be wonderful to hold a
rectangle of paper and chemicals in my hand one rainy winter night by the wood stove and feel the sun of summer on
my face, the ooze of sea mud between my toes, or taste garlic and lemon-drenched crab on my tongue?

As I am snapping and winding, focussing, adjusting the
aperture, changing the f-stop, I feel a constant pull. My
viewpoint is drawn to one central point. I cannot keep
myself from turning the lens toward Peter, framing him as
he tells an off-colour joke to the group lounging beside the
mess of pots and stoves, broken crab shells and empty wine
bottles.

In spite of his fleeting anger with me this afternoon, I
feel hot for him. It must be the weather, this idyllic day. Sun
and sea in certain combinations must surely make any person amorous. I can't be the only one. There is no question
about Mark and Deliah, in their honeymoon suite, a tent
pitched at the cliff edge. And I am certain Paula and Lester
won't be able to help themselves, in their loft under a
moonless sky, Sarah in a stone-heavy sleep on the other side
of the wall.

My eyes follow Peter's hands talking in the air. I love watching him with other people, the animation in his face as he draws them in. The way he puts a hand on their arm as he speaks to them. When he turns his sun toward someone, they feel important, cherished. I know; I bask in his warmth every day. I feel lucky to wrap my arms and legs around his body every night.

After the last guest has left the cove tonight, when we abandon the carcasses of the sacrificed crabs to the seagulls and mink, and Peter carries a sleeping Liam up to the house, I will stay behind for a minute. To imprint this day on the film that runs endlessly through my mind. I might dive again into the silky water and this time gasp with cold as I record in memory the ocean bottom clearly visible below and the absence of the determined child dog-paddling to nowhere. Then I will follow my boys up to the house, to the bedroom where Peter will warm my cold-prickled skin with his hands and I will not be disappointed.

I wonder if Peter paused for a moment today to watch me in the way I watch him. Did he send out a prayer of gratitude to the heavens that he has me? I chide myself for this flickering lack of confidence in his love. I know I am quiet, more reclusive, viewing life from behind the lens of a camera. I know I shed a paler sun.

FIVE

Maggie stopped in West Van village at the big grocery store on the corner. A loaf of bread, a box of tea, canned mushroom soup, a half-dozen apples, a bag of carrots. It was enough. She carried her few purchases to the cashier who, other than a polite greeting, rang them through without a word. Maggie was thankful for the anonymity of the city. If this were the island, the cashier would have asked her about her children, was she starting seedlings for the garden, did she hear about the new baby. People respected your privacy in the city. It was a blessing. She could live her life in quiet solitude. Go for weeks without a conversation with another human. She had her baskets. Who cared if she slept in her car? It wasn't a crime.

She drove the short block across the railway tracks to one of her favourite beaches. Unlike the busy tidal flats at Ambleside Park to the east, where children splashed through stranded pools of lukewarm water and sun worshippers gathered with their dogs, this beach was intimate and comfortable. A hundred metres of pebbles and rock bounded by twin reefs reaching into the water, like arms holding onto the sea. She could always find materials for her baskets here. Kelp and finer seaweeds clung to the coarse face of the reefs, alongside mussels, limpets and whelks in their protective shells. Crabs hid under boulders and barnacles coated any surface. She knew she would have no trouble finding what she wanted.

The tide was low, the beach and reefs exposed. At the upper stretches, before sand transformed to grass and trees and the concrete sidewalk of the city, a higher than usual tide had deposited a line of desiccated seaweed parallel to the shore. It was wet and rank—rotting, twisted rolls of vegetation. Much of the mass was bull kelp.

It was harder to find fresh bull kelp on the beach at this time of year. Summer annuals, the plants grew from tiny polyps on the ocean bottom into kelp forests, where young fish and invertebrates sought shelter among the reproductive fronds that streamed like hair from the gas-filled floats at the surface. After fall and winter storms, the kelp broke away from the bottom, washing up on shore in great snarls like this one. She always took advantage of the winter abundance, gathering carloads of kelp, which she hung to dry from the sunroom ceiling to be reconstituted later in the year.

Sometimes in spring, she might be lucky to find the odd intact plant. Or beach-dried lengths, bleached white by sun and salt. The colour of cured deerskin, they added an attractive effect to her baskets. But today didn't look promising. She stirred the pile with her foot and a swarm of beach hoppers leaped into the air. Useless. Too soft, too damaged, already half decomposed.

Maggie continued down the beach, filling her bags. A

light wind blew in from the water. Ankle-high waves hissed onto the shore. Sand and pebbles stirred under the small power of the curling water. She rarely saw other people at this beach. Today, a child and her mother poked in tide pools on the far reef. The pools were fascinating for children. Blennies and sculpins scooted from crevice to crevice. Gardens of green-feathered anemones lined each pothole and tiny hermit crabs scuttled across the rocky pool bottoms in their borrowed shell homes, their tiny, jointed appendages frantic. Barnacles waved their legs upward to catch tiny bits of detritus from the water column. The little girl squealed. Maggie imagined she might have poked an anemone, as Liam and Joy had loved to do as children, the fleshy tentacles sticking to their fingers.

65

It was a good day; in spite of the lack of bull kelp, the sea goddess had left her many fine materials. A large blanket of Turkish towel, its purple surface covered with tiny bristles; an undamaged rock crab body, the narrow, jointed legs hanging lifeless, pincers no longer threatening. Shells of all kinds and satin-worn driftwood. Plenty of olive-coloured rockweed; her children used to pop the grape-like air bladders with their toes, relishing the snapping sound and the satisfying crunch.

Everything went into her bags, one hanging from each hand. As she walked, they pulled heavily on her arms and she stopped occasionally to rest.

The girl and her mother meandered down the beach toward Maggie. About five, in braids, blue rubber boots and a handmade red wool sweater, the girl reminded Maggie of Joy. For the second time in a few hours, she thought of her daughter. Like this girl, Joy had sucked on her fingers. A feeling of sadness nudged at her and she turned away from the pair, stooping to flip over a rock.

"Come on, Claire," the mother said. The girl had stopped abreast of Maggie. "Time to go, sweetie."

The girl didn't move or answer. Maggie felt the child's innocent gaze on her. The woman turned back, her feet crunching in the gravel, perfume mingling with the tang of seaweed.

"Claire, honey, let's go." The mother's voice was gentle. Maggie stood and half turned toward them. The girl crooked her finger, motioning for her mother to bend down, and whispered in her ear. The woman nodded and, taking the girl's hand, walked the few steps to Maggie.

"Excuse me," she said.

Maggie didn't answer. The woman was in her late twenties, pretty, blonde hair like the girl. She wore expensive jeans, a leather jacket. Maggie imagined she probably drove a Volvo and took the little girl to ballet classes and playgroups. She didn't want to talk to this woman or her daughter.

"My daughter would like you to have this," the woman said. She held out a five-dollar bill. "I know it's not much. I'm sorry. It's all I have with me."

When Maggie didn't move, the woman shifted from foot to foot, then tucked the bill into the top of one of Maggie's bags. It drifted down to settle unseen onto her treasures.

"Well, goodbye." The woman tugged on the girl's hand and they ran down the beach toward the parking lot.

Maggie pulled the bill from the bag. What was that all about? What a strange thing to do. She sat on a driftwood log and smoothed the paper rectangle on her knee. What were they thinking? She noted for the first time the mountain mud caked onto her shoes. Did she look that bad? Her jeans, faded and worn at the knees, were also spattered with mud, her baggy sweater frayed and uneven over her hips.

Thanks to her early-morning abduction to Granville Island, she hadn't brushed her hair since yesterday. In a child's eyes she must appear old, dirty, wandering alone on a beach, filling plastic bags with crabs and seaweed. A bag lady. That's what they thought of her. A lonely old bag lady.

She wanted to get up, run after them and explain. She wanted to open the little girl's hand, laugh with her at the misunderstanding, place the bill in her palm. Tell her to buy herself a toy or ice cream. Show her the shells she was collecting. Take the girl and her mother back to the house and show them the baskets. Give them a basket. Teach them how to make one: how to gather the materials, dry them, weave them together. But the girl and her mother were gone.

Maggie couldn't stand; she didn't trust her legs to hold her. She let the bill fall from her fingers. It settled onto the sand and gravel at her feet. When the weakness passed, she returned to the car and leaned unsteadily against the door. They were mistaken, that pretty little girl and her mother. They had made an assumption, a dreadful assumption. She wasn't a bag lady, a poor, destitute woman, lost to the world. How could they know who she was, what she was thinking? They didn't know her.

Through the window she saw the bedclothes, untidy and accusing in the back seat. "I'm not a bag lady," she yelled to the empty parking lot. But the sack of underwear hanging carelessly across the seat back overwhelmed her with a terrible doubt and she fought back tears. On the beach, the bags of seaweed and shells leaned against the driftwood log, one bag slumping over the corner of the five-dollar bill, now damp and limp with moisture drawn from the sand.

SIX

Maggie walked in the night like a ghost through the house. The dream she had been fleeing had pursued her into the back of the car. The quilt around her naked body was wet with sweat and tears and the cool rain that pattered on the patio doors. The prints of her bare feet followed her across the floor. *Let me out of this place*, she thought, passing by the stacks of baskets that lined the walls of every room. Her feet were icy on the oak floor.

When she reached the bedroom, she switched on the lamp and stood in front of the mirror that stretched across the wall above the vanity. Her eyes gradually adjusted to the light, her image emerging as if from a fog. She drew in her breath at the sight of herself, eyes wild and stricken, framed by a knotted mass of grey-streaked hair. Had she become a crazy woman, haunted by love past? Maggie closed her eyes and reached for the hairbrush on the dresser, feeling for the rough bristles. She pulled it through her hair until she was sure all the tangles were gone before she dared open her eyes. The light and the brushing helped, but her eyes were sunken and ringed with dark shadows, her forehead deeply furrowed. She traced the heavy lines marking her brow, and ran her fingers through her hair; coarse, silvered strands intermingled with the red-brown of her youth. She let the quilt fall from her shoulders to the floor, where it curled in a soft pile at her feet. She had not seen herself naked in the mirror since Peter died. She had no reason. There was no one to appear for.

Maggie's fingers followed the slope of her neck, the skin loose and textured like ripples of water on fine sand. Like her mother used to have . . . when she was an old woman. Yes, an old woman. These past years, when she wasn't looking, this old woman had erased Maggie and drawn herself. And she let her; she didn't even notice.

Her fingers continued their journey of discovery, of reacquaintance, down her body. She traced the pendulous hang of her breasts, the result of gravity and suckling. Cupping their weight in both hands, she felt the warm, dim memory of a baby's lips. Stretch lines accented the emptiness of the now-useless glands, her nipples hard and pink in a pool of mottled brown areola. She moved her hands to the sagging, flabby bulge of her abdomen. Three babies grew here. Their little, round bums, their elbows and arms and knees rolling across the tight elastic surface, jabbing outwards, wanting to escape. When they did, it was pain and sweat and power, and her belly was never the same. She felt fiercely proud of the scars that marred this dimpled mound where her babies had grown, the stretch marks and the low, flat, Caesarean scar through which Liam had entered the world. The scar was numb to her touch, masking the memory. Another tiny smile curved across her navel from the tube-tying a year after Joy was born. The battle scars of motherhood. Her eyes fell to the wiry, tawny curl of hair between her legs and the thick flesh of her thighs. She hadn't thought about sex for a very long time.

Maggie looked at the basket sitting on the bedside table. A twisting of cedar strips through a bull kelp frame, mussel shells on strands of kelp whip, dangling in a circlet around the top edge. A rough lid of plaited kelp. Red, green, brown and blue, colours of the wild. Two half-melted candles flanked the basket, a spent wooden match discarded in a clay dish beside them. She had used the match to light the candles the night she moved out to the car. Was it a month ago, two months?

A photograph of Peter was tucked into the edge of the mirror. Peter on the island in summer, before the cancer. He sat on the smooth, grey-brown sandstone below the house; ocean water glittered in the corner of the picture. His chest was bare, curling with tendrils of fair hair; his tattered cut-off shorts showed the line between white thigh and tanned leg. He held a sketch pad. Maggie remembered how she had crept up behind the peeling, rust and green limb of an arbutus tree with the camera and surprised him. He was laughing, his sandy hair lightened by the summer sun, thinning on top. Relaxed and happy. It was hard, now, to imagine she and Peter had ever been happy like this. Liam and Rose couldn't know, they were young, a lifetime ahead of them. They couldn't know that Maggie had only the past. The future ... aging and loneliness. *Get over it, get on with life.* They expected too much from her.

Maggie lifted the basket lid. Inside was a box, rough foil over cardboard, burnished gold in colour, twenty point three centimetres high by fifteen point two centimetres wide by ten point six centimetres deep. Those were the exact dimensions. She was absolutely certain, having measured it a hundred times since Peter's death. The first time, a nightmare so familiar it had become an old friend.

The first time. Her fingers had been clumsy and wooden, fumbling through the wicker sewing basket on the cluttered desk in their bedroom for the tape measure. It was a white, plastic tape measure with inches marked in bold, black numbers on one side, and centimetres marked in smaller, delicate type on the other. Snarled in thread at the bottom of the sewing basket. Strands of colour wound around each other like a nest of snakes settled in for a long winter, the tape measure trapped in the middle. She hadn't known what to do. On the edge of tears, she stared at the confused ball. Finally, she noticed her scissors glinting in the bottom of the sewing basket. Wrapped in its own knots of thread. Without a thought, she snipped the threads with her teeth, one by one, until the scissors were free. Why she didn't do the same to free the tape measure, she now can't imagine.

When she had the tape measure loose, she spent the longest time turning it over from one white side to the other. Did it matter, the discrepancy in the size and boldness of the numbers? Would her choice of centimetres or inches say anything about importance? She hadn't wanted to make any mistakes. This measuring, this recording must be perfect, for it would carry the evidence, the proof, of those past few unimaginable days. In the end she chose centimetres, they had seemed more exact, more refined. Peter would have chosen centimetres. Wouldn't he? She measured and remeasured the gold foil box until she was sure she had gotten it right, jotting the numbers into her diary.

The day of measuring was the same day she collected Peter from the crematorium. She went alone, refusing Mark's company. The waiting room of the funeral home was painted in sombre tones, the lighting subdued, the furniture comfortable. Organ music drifted from the walls. A tall man in a dark suit walked towards her down the dimly lit hallway, his face solemn, unsmiling. He carried the box in two hands like it was a crown on a velvet cushion. The set of his shoulders, the slow, halting measure of his pace, held an odd sense of misplaced ceremony. He laid the box in her lap; she almost expected him to congratulate her on this honour. But his eyes were sympathetic. He pulled a sheaf of papers from an envelope. Put a pen in her trembling hand. Pulled a table to her knees. She signed the forms, affirming she belonged to this little box. How could she know for sure? There was not even a label to assure her.

73

Later at home, alone in the bedroom, she opened it, not daring to breathe for fear she would blow ash into the air. Instead of ash, she found a white cloud of cotton, like clothes-drier lint, stuffed in the top. She pulled it out bit by bit like a magician pulling out handkerchief after handkerchief from his pocket. Was her husband in there? Had the undertakers forgotten him? Or, hope of hopes, this was a terrible dream and she would wake up to find Peter snoring beside her, covers bunched at his feet, one arm flung across her chest.

At last, the cotton came free and she gasped at the amount of ash in the container—two litres at most. So little. She had imagined it to be like fireplace ash, coarse flakes of grey, black and white. But here was a fine dust, finer than powdered sugar, the constant grey of heavy rain on a Vancouver mid-winter day. It smelled like garden soil, heaped into mounds against the sides of the box. Silent and ethereal. A dusting of heaven fallen to earth. If she had taken her finger, reached down in and touched it, she was sure it would be like touching air, a breath on her fingertip, a hint of an idea. But what would she disturb? A molecule of femur, a neuron, the piece of his heart that said, "I love you, Maggie"? She was afraid. She couldn't bear to release a single particle into the winds of time. She wanted all of him. She shoved the cotton lint back in the box, replaced the lid and cradled the tiny package in her arms. She swore through her tears that she would never open it again.

She never had.

Until now. Three years later. Maggie knew the patina of the box by heart. It was a bit worn, like herself, from the heartache of the past few years. The foil, tarnished like an aged brass pot, had peeled away at the corners, and the top was dented and scratched in places. Hot tears had left a pattern curiously like a bird in flight across one corner. All that measuring and holding and crying.

Maggie pulled on her housecoat and picked up the ashes. She walked through the house to the sunroom. Switching on the light, she surveyed the stacks of baskets. Each had been crafted with one purpose: to contain the soul of a man who wanted to be free.

Except one. There was one basket Maggie had made without Peter in mind. She put Peter's box onto the work table and climbed a stool beside the wall cupboard. Standing on her toes, she peered onto the top shelf. It was still there. It hadn't disintegrated as she had thought it might. She slid it off the shelf. A cascade of dust and seaweed flakes fell onto her sleeve. She turned it around in the light of the ceiling lamp. This basket had been a failure. A loose frame of knotted kelp whip draped with sheets of sea lettuce—*Ulva*. Paper-thin and fragile. She should have known it was impossible. The sheets had cracked as they dried. Some had fallen apart completely. The colour had faded from grass-green to dull grey. But she had loved the process. The challenge of transforming such a fragile material into a basket. To give it more time on this earth.

Maggie carried the basket to the table and set it beside the foil box. It wasn't the only failure. The compost bin in the garden was full of broken and incomplete baskets. It had been lovely for a while. At first, the fine sheets of moist algae were opaque like stained glass, and a candle had cast a warm glow through the glistening emerald walls. She had wanted to show it to Joy. Joy had watched her make it. But she never got the opportunity. Joy was gone. And the basket so dusty and sad-looking she couldn't show it to anyone.

Maggie pushed it to the back of the table and picked up the gold foil box. With trembling hands she pried off the lid, pulled the stuffing free and peered in at the drifts of ash. She had an important question to ask her husband.

Ulva
SEA LETTUCE

It takes time and concentration to make a basket. I gather materials from the beach and the forest, seeking perfection. I leave behind the chipped mussel shells, the crab exoskeletons with only one claw, the cracked and broken cockles. I won't take anything with spots of rot: a rope of bull kelp turning soft, a brittle strip of cedar, a damp feather. Because they won't last. There is great danger in using these once-live materials, for living and dying are merely a paper-thin space of time apart. Without care, without the precise humidity, the exact amount of sun, without the perfect amount of time, my baskets might fall apart. They might decompose to a pile of humus. I would be left with nothing.

I am making one now, a large basket of bull kelp. The metres of tapering bull kelp stipe are perfect for the foundation of baskets. When dried, the float end can be thick and round as an arm, the holdfast end as fine and strong as cord. I am using cuttings from the middle section, three fingers thick and varying in colour from white to cinnamon.

The float will make a perfect handle. If I plan it right, it will be dark and light interwoven into a checkerboard pattern. Perhaps I will adorn it with clumps of mussel shells and a few rufous hummingbird feathers. The iridescent green of the feathers will be exquisite against the blue of the shells and the warm glow of the kelp when it's dry. I am lucky to have these feathers. Not lucky for the bird, though. Liam found it dead by the feeder in the garden. Its neck was broken. It must have flown into the patio doors.

78

I spend every day in the sunroom making baskets, or outside collecting materials. It makes me forget; keeps me from thinking about Peter. I hardly notice that Joy is gone now. First Liam, now Joy gone. Goodness knows they don't want to be here with me.

Last week I was working on a delicate basket. An experiment—thin sheets of sea lettuce, *Ulva*, set whole and damp in a dry, loose frame of fine kelp whip. I had a notion it would make a lovely lantern, candlelight shining through the walls. But sea lettuce is delicate, a mere two cells thick. It tears easily; I have to be extra careful. I was placing the first sheet of *Ulva* into the kelp form when I heard footsteps down the hall. They stopped in the doorway.

"Mom?" It was Joy.

I didn't answer. I was annoyed at the interruption. I didn't want this basket ruined. I'd never made one like it before.

"Mother." Her voice was louder.

I looked up. "Not right now, Joy."

She growled and crossed her arms. She had always been strong-willed. But so precious as an infant. So precious . . . after Angel. Peter named her Joy; he said she was a gift. But she's not little anymore. She's sixteen. She's changed. She wears nothing but black. Black army pants, baggy black

sweaters, black socks, big black boots, black, black, black.
And her hair. Her beautiful auburn hair. It's gone. She's cut
if off. Bleached and dyed what's left. It was green that day.
Probably purple the next. She looks like a prison inmate.
Five earrings in each ear and one in her nose. I couldn't
bear the sight of her.

"You were such a sweet baby," I said as I returned to my
work.

"Baby. What are you talking about? I'm not a baby anymore, Mother. Look at me. I'm sixteen. I'm a woman. Look
at me," Joy yelled.

"I'll be finished in a half hour or so, Joy, then I'll talk to
you."

"I can't wait half an hour, Mother. I can't stand this anymore. I need you to listen to me. Now!"

But I couldn't listen. I had to pay attention to what I was
doing. It was time to place the next piece.

"Mother, I've been living in this house with you, watching you like this, making your baskets, those stupid baskets,
and I'm going crazy. Do you even know I'm here?"

I picked up a pair of tweezers to catch up the lime green
sheets from the tray where they had been drying. They were
flexible enough to bend within the bull kelp frame. It looked
like it was going to work. I was excited. Perhaps I would use
this basket for something other than Peter's ashes.

"Maybe you'd notice me if I was dead like Dad." Joy had
stopped screaming. Her voice was measured, deliberate.

I couldn't listen to such nonsense. The timing for the
basket was critical. I had to force myself to stay calm with
Joy. She was always the drama queen. Peter and I thought
she would make a good actress. He had been more tolerant
of her theatrics. I found it better to ignore her when she
talked this way.

"Maybe you could just strangle me with one of those long seaweeds. Put me out of my misery," Joy went on. "Mother. I'm moving out. I'm going to live with Uncle Mark. Did you hear me?" She was yelling again. "I'm moving out!"

I swivelled around to get a piece of tissue to dab excess moisture from the basket and caught sight of her. She wore her storm-cloud face. Peter's name for the scowl that meant she was spitting mad. He liked to tease her. It only made things worse. I couldn't figure out what else I read in her face, a bunch of mixed-up emotions. I couldn't begin to make the effort to figure them out. I was too tired. I turned back to my work.

"Don't you care, Mother?" She didn't wait for an answer. Just stomped away in her black boots and slammed the door so hard the windows rattled.

The next day she didn't come to breakfast. I walked down the hallway to her bedroom. Her door was open, her clothes gone.

Mark came in the late afternoon. He leaned against the door frame of the sunroom, fiddling with the edge of his fleece jacket while I worked.

"Did you know Joy is over at our place?" he asked.

"Yes, she said something about it yesterday," I said.

"She wants to live with us," he said. "She says she's never coming back here. What happened, Maggie?"

"You know Joy," I said. "Over-dramatizing everything."

"Yeah, I know Joy." He took a step toward me. "I know she misses her dad like hell and she's dying for some attention from her mother."

"Don't be silly," I said. "I've always been here for her."

He pulled at his scruffy beard. "Physically, maybe. At least you're in the house. But you might as well be . . . Maggie, Joy is a young woman. She needs her mother. Is this what you want? For her to move out?"

He shoved his hands into the front pockets of his jeans. He was looking at me like everyone else did. Like I was crazy. I felt irritated with him. Surely he could understand the situation. He worked with teenagers. He knew what they could be like.

"Yes, she is growing up," I snapped. "And she always knew what she wanted. God help me if I step in her way. It's best, Mark, I think. She loves you. And Deliah. She can help out with the kids. And don't worry, I'll give you money. How much do you want? You can have her family allowance cheque."

Mark straightened up and ran his hand through his black curls.

"God, Maggie. This isn't about money. I'm happy to have her. But—"

"It'll do us good to have some time apart. You know we've always bashed heads. Besides, she'll come home when she's ready. Now, if you don't mind, I've got work to do."

He stood silently for a minute more, then said, "I hope you're right, Maggie." And left.

Over the next couple of days, the rest of Joy's belongings disappeared: her bed, her stuffed animal collection, the picture of Peter from her desk—gone. They must have come with Mark's van while I was out collecting. Joy didn't say goodbye. But I'm not worried. She'll get over it. She always does.

SEVEN

The drive along the causeway to the Tsawassen ferry terminal always made Maggie feel like she was driving off the edge of the world. The terminal hung on the end of a finger spit of land jutting into the Strait of Georgia, bounded on one side by a gravel and sand beach and by black mud flats on the other. It felt odd to drive out into the water to board a boat, as if the ferries needed a jump-start to reach the islands visible to the west. Today, a couple of dozen herons foraged on stick legs in the flats and the trains at the neighbouring coal docks at Roberts Bank looked like toys, dwarfed by the loading cranes and the foreign freighters alongside.

Maggie paid her fare at the ticket booth and parked behind a battered Ford pick-up at the end of the line of Gulf Island ferry traffic. The terminal was crowded. The Gulf Island ferry, the old *Queen of Tsawassen*, was in the middle of the Strait and Maggie judged it would be at the dock in about ten minutes.

Maggie turned off the car and slapped her palms against the steering wheel. She would like to take Liam over her knee right now and give him a good smack! She could never do it, though; she had never hit either of her children, never given herself that choice. But she couldn't deny the urge was there. He had managed to win again. She was tempted to slip her car out of line and head back to the highway. In the passenger seat, Peter in his basket was buckled in safely. He wouldn't approve of a change of heart and a mad dash for the exit, would he? She reached over and brushed a dusting of dirt off the edge of the basket. Through the cracks between the kelp warp, the foil of the box glowed like unearthed treasure. She couldn't get over the fact that a grown man, broad-shouldered, size ten and a half feet, could be reduced to a cardboard container the size of a shoebox.

She peered furtively behind her. Several more cars had arrived and she was trapped in the middle of a long column of waiting vehicles. Escape was impossible. She caught sight of a paper bag lying on its side in the back seat. Inside was the sea lettuce basket. She had thrown it in at the last minute, unsure of why she felt the need to bring it. A vague notion that she could fix it? A sense of pity for the broken, dejected failure? It would likely spend the entire trip composting in the back of the car.

The car stank of cigarettes and a thick, sweet odour she couldn't place ... marijuana? The seats were threadbare, the floors caked with mud, the windshield cracked. She knew if she crouched down to see under the seat there would be crumpled chocolate bar wrappers, empty pop cans and who knows what else. But it was better than driving down the island in her old station wagon. Everybody would recognize it. On the island, people waved or tipped a finger up off the steering wheel when meeting a car, any car, strange or familiar. Everyone knew all the local cars. And the driver's business . . . or thought they did.

When she refused to bring her own car, Liam had negotiated a week-long trade from a friend. This wreck would fit right in with the island culture; a rural car, scraped and dented, a dozen splotches of touch-up paint along the body. She was glad the muffler didn't roar; it would be too conspicuous, draw too much attention.

Attention was something Maggie wanted to avoid. She had wrapped her hair in a green kerchief and, despite an overcast sky, she wore dark glasses. In the parking lot, people chatted in groups of two or three. She recognized most of them, locals from Galiano. Islanders returning from a trip to town, doing their 'list', which hung from a clip on the dashboard of the car. Each item on the list would have a matching check mark, and if it didn't, would be added to next week's list. She knew their cars were bulging with groceries, big packages of toilet paper, parts for tools, hay for the horse, anything not available on the island. Maggie had never finished a list in one day. Hers had gone on forever and ever, the way she had imagined her life on the island would do.

Three vehicles ahead, a man leaned against his door, smoking and talking with another man and two women. Beside them, two children threw a ball to a black Lab on a leash. The man near the car was Lyle Madsen. He managed the lumberyard; his wife had run off with one of the truck drivers and left him with four young children to raise. The children with the dog? It was hard to tell, Maggie hadn't seen anyone from the island since Peter's town funeral. They might be Lyle's youngest two; they should be ten or twelve by now. What were their names? Anna and Sam?

One of the women was Tina Smith; she lost both breasts to cancer when she was fifty. Tom Brandon, the second man, had a record for bank robbery; he was a pretty famous potter now. On the island, when you looked at a person, you didn't see their physical body, you saw their life story. Maggie used to find it comforting to know that people here knew each other intimately, accepted one another in spite of their differences. But today and for the next week, she wanted to remain invisible and unknown.

"Damn, there's Agnes Cruikshanks." Maggie slouched down in the seat and adjusted her glasses as the second woman turned and sauntered along the line of cars. She was short and stout, her complexion ruddy, her silver perm tight against her head. She looked like a bee in a bright yellow shawl draped over an orange and black pantsuit. Like a bee she flitted up to every car, leaned into the window and buzzed, Maggie knew, with gossip. If Agnes spotted her the whole island would know she was here.

Maggie could imagine the conversation. Agnes, loud and jolly, leaning through the open window, her sharp, black eyes darting around the car, snooping. "Why, Maggie Cooper, how are you, dear? It's been years. So sorry about Peter and. . . ." Unspoken: *I want all the grisly details about how he died, how the cancer cells moved like thieves through his body until they had stolen the last breath from him.* . . . "How are little Joy and young Liam? What! Graduated? Twenty-three! Why, isn't it amazing how quickly they grow?"

It was inevitable she would see the basket and Maggie would be stuck, trying to explain she was on her way to the island to fling the ashes of her husband into the freezing ocean, to float on the currents to whoever knows where and she'd never be able to keep track of him.

As Agnes came abreast of Maggie's car, the loading announcement for the ferry blared out over the parking lot and, with a curious glance at Maggie's mysterious figure in the unknown vehicle, she turned away. Maggie sent up a word of thanks to the owner of the rattletrap. No one on the island would recognize it, even Agnes Cruikshanks.

The lineup snaked onto the narrow loading ramp and into the gaping mouth of the ferry. Maggie hesitated. She glanced over her shoulder. She could still get out of here. The orange-vested attendant ran forward and waved at her; an impatient honk sounded from behind. Maggie fumbled with her keys, then drove into the belly of the ship. The ship's whistle sounded and the steel doors rolled closed behind her. Through the narrowing gap between the doors, she could see a flock of gulls circling behind the boat, diving into the wake in hopes of a few tidbits of food. Ahead, she knew the low green-grey silhouette of the islands waited across the Strait. No turning back now.

The islanders climbed from their cars, doors slamming. Maggie knew they were going up to the coffee shop to continue their conversations. She used to be one of them, anxious to catch up on the lives of her friends. They would knit and talk for the entire hour-long voyage while their children played cards or games of make-believe on the floor.

Maggie also knew that once the ferry docked at the Sturdies Bay ferry terminal, the islanders would head for the General Store. In the back room, they would drink more coffee and chat with whomever happened to be around before heading home with a few groceries, the supplies from town and juicy tidbits of hearsay. The General Store was an icon of rural sociability, a throwback from decades ago. It was one room, cozy and cluttered. The plank floors were dark with oil and age; baskets and boxes of fruits and vegetables surrounded a pot-bellied stove in the middle of the room. The storekeepers kept shop behind a glass cooler from which you could choose a slab of bacon or a cut of cheese wrapped in butcher's paper. In the rear corner of the store was the back room, separated from the place of commerce by a glass-bead curtain that tinkled as you walked through. The back room was always full of people, particularly on market day, sitting in chairs and benches around an airtight stove. Driftwood plank shelves filled with tattered paperbacks, old bottles and a collection of glass Japanese fishing balls lined the walls. The prop of an old airplane hung from the ceiling. The proprietor was an avid pilot of antique biplanes. The conversation was public, shared among all in the room, and, of course, it stopped abruptly when a stranger clinked through the bead curtain.

It had taken Maggie two years to enter the back room of the General Store. Paula convinced her she was silly. One Friday in January, the two of them, both heavily pregnant with their first children, walked into the store. Paula, huge and bold, stopped at the counter and ordered two mugs of ginger tea. Maggie followed her past the cashiers and through the curtain. The beads jingled and clacked behind them. Everyone stopped talking and turned to survey the newcomers. A bearded man in the corner made a joke about an alien invasion by beach balls. The woman beside him laughed and everyone joined in. Paula and Maggie looked at each other and broke into a fit of giggles. People shuffled about and made room for them on the padded bench. Maggie felt she had made it into island society, although people went out of their way to remind her it took twenty years to earn the official title of islander. It became a market-day ritual to meet Paula for tea in the back room.

Today, though, she had no intention of visiting the General Store. She would drive right by, incognito.

Maggie was shocked when she drove through Sturdies Bay to discover the General Store had changed hands. It had fresh paint, a new sign advertising cappuccino, and people lounged at round wooden tables on an outside deck. Next door was a new mini-mall with a bakery and a takeout shop. It had been years since she'd been on the island—what did she expect? The world hadn't stopped in her absence.

89

Nobody tipped a finger at Maggie the entire half-hour drive from the ferry dock to the cove. She didn't see a single car along the twelve kilometres of road. The road, paved but rough and narrow, curved through forest, lined to the narrow shoulder by graceful western red cedar and thick-barked Douglas-fir trees. Delicate swaths of fresh stinging nettle filled the ditches. She had always loved this drive. There were no traffic lights or stop signs. It relaxed her after the busy city. It was green, all year 'round. Not simply green, but a dozen shades of it. Peter had told the children green was the most relaxing colour, which was why God painted the island a million shades of it.

A deer crossed the road ahead. She braked and pulled onto the grass shoulder. The animal flashed its white tail and bounded into the trees. She waited a moment for a following fawn or two, but it was early; the tiny, spotted creatures would be curled up, hidden in the forest. Ahead of the car, a wooden sign hung beside a dirt road angling into the forest. Fletcher's Range Eggs. Paula's road. Beautiful Paula with her long blonde braids swinging past her waist and adventure in her eye. They'd been best friends. Maggie had automatically turned down this road whenever she was out in the car, bumping the ten minutes of ungravelled track to the clearing where Paula and her family raised chickens. Maggie and Paula spent many hot, summer days in the shade of the giant maple outside Paula's back door, drinking fresh lemonade or, sometimes, home-brewed beer, chickens clucking and scratching around their feet. The children splashed naked in the plastic pool. When Liam and Sarah were toddlers, they packed them on their backs and hiked the high backbone ridge that ran the length of the island. Paula knew most of the plants; she studied botany in Victoria before she married Lester. The two women gathered wild onion on the dry cliff sides and dock in the moist shade of the east forest. Paula always had strange herbal concoctions brewing on her stove and she knew what to do for any ailment. Any ailment—except Maggie's grief.

The last time Maggie saw Paula was the day of Peter's funeral in Vancouver. Paula arrived with a dozen other islanders and a huge wreath made of fall foliage. After the ceremony she pulled Maggie to her and cried, rocking back and forth. Maggie couldn't bring herself to hug her back. Paula was happiness, the happiness of the island ... of Peter.

For months after the funeral, Paula called every week and left message after message. Maggie stood beside the phone listening to her patient voice. She came to the Vancouver house a couple of times and stood at the door, ringing and knocking. From the end of the hall, Maggie could see Paula's statuesque profile through the blue haze of the stained glass in the front door. One day Paula walked around the house, peering into windows before she gave up and drove away. There were at least a dozen letters. Maggie burned them unread in the stone fireplace in the living room. The calls and letters came less frequently and after a time stopped altogether.

Maggie stepped on the gas pedal, looking over her shoulder at the sign one more time before she continued down the main road.

There had also been a memorial service on the island for Peter. Joy and Liam had come over with Mark. In spite of their begging, she had refused to join them. She knew how it would be; she had been to other island memorials like it. The community hall decorated with wreaths of moss and leaves and rosehips; a large one on the front door encircling a photo of Peter. The floor strewn with autumn leaves, the walls and stage crowded with flowers, the metal stacking chairs arranged in neat rows, an aisle down the middle. A table near the kitchen would sag under the weight of home baking, potluck style. The smell of perking coffee would waft from the stainless steel urn in the serving window. There would be standing room only; people would spill down the front steps and onto the road. It was always the same. Every person on the island came to a memorial. People would stand in the service and say nice things about Peter, what a talented illustrator and patient teacher he was, an example to the community, a wonderful father, a valued volunteer with the fire department. Afterward, while the men stacked the chairs against the wall, the women served coffee and pie with ice cream and the young children ran in and out, panting and red-cheeked from a game of tag or Red Rover in the meadow beside the hall. The event would be too friendly, everyone lining up to hug her and offer a few words of condolence.

Maggie stayed in bed that day.

She parked at the end of the gravel road and stepped out of the car into sunshine and the stiff odour of salt and kelp. A canopy of bigleaf maple trees towered overhead and the path to the beach was lined with head-high thimbleberry. Her stomach was tight with unease at being in these familiar surroundings. She almost turned and ran back to the car. *Damn you, Liam!* she thought. Why did she let him talk her into this?

The old red canoe hung in its usual perch, two curved branches of a large tree above the beach. She struggled to lift it down. The tree had grown thicker over the years and the gunwale of the boat was wedged in the U-shaped crook. The tide was low and she dragged the canoe to the water's edge across the barnacle-coated rocks, cringing at the rough scrape against the boat's hull. Peter had always insisted they carry it. She looked at the basket in the bottom of the canoe. But he wasn't here now, was he?

Loading her pack with as much gear as she could carry, she stowed it in the bow and pushed off from the beach with the maplewood paddle she had brought along. Liam's paddle . . . a birthday present from Peter. He had hand-planed and sanded it for days in his workshop below the house until the surface was like silk. He hadn't wrapped it, simply handed it shiny with new varnish into Liam's eager hands. The varnish was dull now and curled in flakes from the blade.

A slight breeze stirred the water of the cove, sunlight reflecting off each little wave. This was one of the few safe harbours on the southwest side of Galiano Island. In summer, there were two or three sailboats anchored here each night, but now it was empty. The shell and mud beach was the single easy water access.

Maggie inhaled deeply at the sight of the island; its familiar profile, a mound of beige rock and spiky green forest, floated in a bowl of blue-green ocean. It was more a fragment of Galiano than a separate entity, like a clinging child unwilling to part more than a step away from Mother. At an extreme low tide Maggie and the children used to wade through the sludge of mud and eelgrass between the island and Galiano and never get their knees wet. Joy, who had a name for everything, used to call them Mother and Baby Island. "Are we going to the Mother Island to get groceries now?" she would ask. "I must give Baby Island a hug so it doesn't get lonely." She would fling herself face down onto the ground and spread her arms wide, kissing the moss, rocks and dirt with great ceremony. A wave of nostalgia broke over Maggie's shoulders and she blinked back tears as she plunged the paddle into the sea.

In reality, the island had no name. Most of the other islands scattered throughout the Strait of Georgia, even the rocky islets that barely raised their heads over a high tide, had names like Tree, Canoe and Rose. It had been unnamed when Peter's grandfather bought it and the family had left it that way. A name to them denoted ownership. They considered themselves caretakers of a precious piece of nature. Maggie wondered if the new owners would give the island a name.

Both children had grown up here. Like intertidal creatures, they spent their lives at the beach searching for crabs and fishing for tide pool sculpins. Or like wood nymphs with their secret tree huts and trails through the woods adults were not supposed to know about.

Baby Island seemed lonely as Maggie guided the canoe alongside the dock, which was empty but for the rowboat overturned on the rough planking. The sign—PRIVATE ISLAND—hung from a piling, weatherworn and faded, spattered with gull droppings. The railings of the ramp needed painting. Like Liam's paddle, everything appeared neglected. She took the steep walk up the wooded trail to the house in measured steps, the knot in her belly tightening.

Her feet followed the trail out of habit. She had walked it many times in the dark of night with one child or the other asleep in her arms. Not once had she stumbled or missed a turn, her feet guided by the subtle changes in the path itself.

A handful of withered tulips, the bulbs planted when the children were small, drooped at the side of the trailhead. Few wildflowers grew on the dark, damp, northeast side of the island. Fir trees and red huckleberry, Saskatoon, high banks of salal and shrubs of false box massed the sloping ground calf-deep in moss. The other side, the open southwest, would be resplendent with spring colour, terraces of meadows like waterfalls of flowers running down to the sea.

As she crested the top of the hill, she saw the house below her, bordered by the river of wildflowers. She paused at the top of the rock staircase leading down to the bench of land where the house was perched. From her vantage point at the height of the island, it was hard to believe the house didn't tumble from the cliffside into the water. It was more integrated with the island than she recalled. The cedar shakes covering the roof had silvered with age, blending with the lichen-stained siding and the foliage of the three, giant, windswept firs growing through the decks, so that Maggie doubted it could be seen from the channel against the backdrop of sandstone and forest. The walls were mostly glass. Even from here she could see clear through the house to the trees and water beyond. Birds often flew into the expanse of glass and black cardboard crows had been mounted in each window to warn away flickers and robins.

She and Peter had spent days walking the island, hunting for the perfect house site. They had always come back to this meadow. The views were stunning in all directions: to the west a maze of islands and the mountains of Vancouver

Island, to the south and southwest the low, comforting hills of Saltspring Island, the open run of Trincomali Channel to the southeast, and to the north and east the green of dense forest. This house had been a labour of love. Every board, each nail, post and tile had come to the island in the rowboat, hauled up the trail by tractor. Never before had she felt like an artist, a creator of permanence. She thought she would never leave.

95

Maggie walked down the rock stairway to the deck, unlocked the French doors and stepped inside. Her footsteps echoed around the empty house. No merry shrieks of happy children, no laughter, no music. No smells of cooking, the house was swept clean of any evidence of living.

She dropped her pack on the counter. Cradling Peter's basket, she walked through the rooms, running her hand along the countertops, the walls, pulling the memories in through her fingertips, to connect once again with her former home.

It was small, only a handful of rooms. Cedar posts supported solid square beams and a ceiling high and expansive, lined with skylights. The kitchen, living room and master bedroom wrapped around a great stone chimney. No doors save to the bathroom. A white enamel cookstove and a black cast-iron airtight in the master bedroom were the only heat sources. A set of stairs at the end of the kitchen led to the children's loft. Everywhere you looked, windows framed the shifting character of the ocean, the oak and arbutus meadows and the forest. The light was amazing; it had been like living within a crystal ball, the future always clear.

Maggie followed the hallway past the bathroom to a short stairway leading to the master bedroom, which doubled as a library. This had been the heart of the house, where she and Peter had slept, dreamed, loved, cried and talked. It had also been the room where Peter worked, his drawing table overlooking the channel. It was her favourite room, the walls lined with bookshelves, the bed built high into a windowed alcove.

She took the first step down into the room and stopped, startled. Someone—a man—was sitting at Peter's drawing table, his back towards her, head bowed in concentration. He wore a faded pair of sweatpants and a blue sweatshirt. His greying blond hair curled to the collar of his shirt. From behind, he looked just like Peter.

Maggie leaned heavily against the wall, her head spinning at the scene. The familiar profile, the arm moving methodically over the paper, an open bottle of ink on the table beside him. He paused and dipped his pen into the inkpot.

"Excuse me," Maggie said, her throat tight and her mouth dry. The man continued to work.

"Peter?" Her voice faltered.

She stepped onto the next tread. Her ankle wrenched sideways and she fell, crying out in pain. She flung both arms forward to brace her fall. The basket flew from her hands and into the air, bouncing onto the floor. Her cheek against the cold, smooth wood, Maggie watched the foil box tumble from the upturned basket, the lid fall open. Ashes spilled across the pale, blond grains of hemlock, like water, flowing fingers of ash spreading out in tiny waves. A cloud of fine dust floated above the scene of the liberation. Maggie scrambled across the floor on her hands and knees, grunting with panic. She fumbled in her pocket for a tissue. Frantically, but with painstaking care, she brushed the pool of ash back into the foil box, lifting each minute particle. A single eyelash must not be lost. When she was sure she had gotten it all, she stuffed the tissue into the box and closed the lid. Her heart banged in her chest, out of control. Why had she come here? Who was this man? Why had she fallen?

She knew she hadn't merely fallen, she had tripped. Or been tripped. But the step was empty.

The chair at the drawing table was also empty. The man was gone. Maggie pulled herself to her feet and hobbled, her ankle throbbing, to the table. Except for a single sheet of paper, it was bare. She picked up the paper. She could barely hold it in her shaking hand. The drawing was a landscape, a forest grove. A half-circle of massive firs, a sweep of ferns, a carpet of moss, a nurse log sprouting a half-dozen hemlock seedlings. And in the lower right corner, the familiar initials P.L.C.

Maggie gripped the edge of the drawing table to steady herself from the wave of dizziness that washed over her. She lowered herself to the floor. The tenants must have found it and left it on the desk. She held the paper to her nose and drew in the thick, pungent odour of permanent ink. The signature smudged black onto her fingertip. This man couldn't have been Peter. It was impossible.

A hesitant knock sounded from the kitchen. Flustered, she pulled herself to standing and limped over to the steps where she could see down the hallway to the kitchen door. A man stood on the deck dressed in jeans, t-shirt and faded denim jacket. He peered through the glass, squinting. Maggie ducked back around the corner but it was too late. He waved and opened the door.

"Hello? Mrs. Cooper?" he said.

Maggie stepped from her hiding place and shuffled up the stairs into the hall. "Yes, I'm Mrs. Cooper." She could see him more clearly. It wasn't the same man. His clothes were wrong. He was too stocky, his hair dark.

"Sorry to bother you. I wasn't sure if you were expecting me," he said, "but Dan Collier asked me to come by and fix the rock stairway down to the garden. I'm Alan Page."

"Oh," she said. "I didn't know. I . . . I guess you should go ahead and do it."

Maggie kept her distance, reluctant to show this stranger her tear-blotched face and her limp.

"Thanks." He started to close the door, stopped and gazed around the kitchen. "Beautiful place. I often paddle my kayak past the island and wondered what the house was like. You can hardly see it from the water."

When Maggie didn't offer any reply, he said, "Well, I'd better get to work." He closed the door and walked across the deck to the stairs down to the garden.

"Wait!" Maggie hopped across the kitchen on one foot and yanked open the door. "Wait! Were—were you here, I mean, in the house a few moments ago?"

He stopped walking and turned, frowning. "No, I just got here. Why, is everything okay?"

"Yes, everything is . . . fine," she lied. "I thought I heard a noise. I guess I'm not used to the quiet."

"I know what you mean," he said. "It took me a while to appreciate the peace. But I'm afraid I'll be making my fair share of noise for a few days. If it bothers you, just let me know. And if you need any help with anything, don't hesitate to ask."

"Yes, thanks. But I'm sure everything will be all right," Maggie said.

"Well, see you later." Alan took the stairs down to the garden two at a time.

Maggie stood in the open door. A flock of pine siskins skittered through the oak grove beyond the deck. The house no longer seemed empty. It was teeming with strange men. She pulled her sweater tight around her shoulders. She hoped the garden job would be a quick one.

Cytisus scoparius
SCOTCH BROOM

Sometimes, when I am around Peter, I feel like an unfinished painting that doesn't live up to his standards. It's not
anything he does. It's the way he says things, out of the
blue.

Today we were working behind the house, clearing Scotch
broom. I hate this weed. It takes over any disturbed ground.
It doesn't belong here. A homesick Scotsman brought it to
the islands, and it has become a nuisance. When we moved
to the island, the meadows were overgrown with it, the
slopes down to the sea yellow with its blossoms right through
from spring to late summer. You could hear the seed pods
snap in the heat, tossing millions more seeds onto the
ground. My friend Paula tells me broom is good for the soil.
It fixes nitrogen, she says. If we left it for a long time it would
eventually give way to native vegetation. But I've seen land
where it has grown unbounded. A broom forest follows the
power lines that cut like a wound across Galiano on their
way to Vancouver Island. The plants are the size of trees,

the trunks as thick as a man's leg. It would take a chainsaw to cut them down.

We clear it from the island every year, pulling the tiny seedlings and cutting the bigger plants. We burn the branches and seedlings in big piles, or throw them into the sea. The wildflowers are more abundant now. Last year I found chocolate lilies in the high grass near the tractor shed. It's working. I feel satisfied after a day of pulling broom. Like I have made a real difference in the world, at least this beautiful three-hectare world.

Not today. I feel like faulty merchandise. I thought we were having a wonderful afternoon together. Early June can be wet, but the day was dry and clear, the sun warm like summer should be. I put Liam in his basket on the back deck where I could see him. He usually sleeps a couple of hours after lunch. Besides, he can barely roll over.

It was a rare moment. Peter and I alone, working side by side, not speaking, comfortable with each other. Peter had the big loppers. He cut the large, coarse, broom stems off above the ground and let them fall. I followed behind, stacking them into mounds. I love watching him work. It doesn't matter if he is sitting at his drawing table, doing the dishes, splitting firewood or pulling broom. He has a graceful way of moving his body like a dancer, no wasted energy. His muscles worked under his t-shirt, a film of sweat on his temples. Knowing I am his and he is mine gives me a warm, delicious feeling.

We knew not to remove the big roots. Raw ground was an invitation to broom seeds to sprout. My job was to pull the new green shoots of the year, before they had a chance to establish. Most of them slipped easily from the ground; the bigger seedlings took more effort. It was hot work, but we were making progress. In an hour we had a pile as high as I could reach, ready to burn in the fall.

The adult eagles were watching us. Regal, perched on a snag, one above the other, white heads motionless, black eyes following our every move. I have always thought of them as king and queen of the island, and we the peons, tending their land for them. That's how I think of us, care-takers of this small wonder.

That's what I was thinking when Peter turned to me, the loppers dangling from one gloved hand. He looked annoyed, his eyebrows arched, his face streaked with dirt.

"I don't know what you're thinking," he said.

It wasn't a question. "What are you thinking?" It was an accusation, like I wasn't pulling the broom correctly. Like I wasn't thinking loud enough for him to hear me. I was puzzled.

"I don't know what you mean, Peter," I said, laughing weakly, embarrassed.

"I've been watching you, trying to figure out what you were thinking. And I couldn't do it." He frowned. "I can usually tell what the people around me are thinking. Most people are preoccupied with one thing or other. It's obvi-ous. I mean, don't you know when you are in the General Store that old Fred is thinking about the glass of whiskey he's going to have when he gets home? Or my brother Mark, he's plotting that great Canadian novel he's always talking about writing. Even Liam, I can tell you right now he's dreaming about a milk break. What are you thinking about, Maggie? I thought I should know." He shook his head and, not waiting for an answer, turned and walked away.

"I . . . I was thinking. About the eagles—" I blurted out in my own defense; my words trailed off to nothing. But he didn't hear me, he was gone, the loppers over his shoulder, to the next patch of broom down the path, unaware of the wound he had inflicted on me with his casual comment, his moment of philosophizing, his misunderstanding.

The eagles took flight at that moment, as if bored with my petty human tragedy. No telltale motion, no chatter to one another before they opened their wings in perfect unison and soared from their perches. Did they know one another's every thought?

Liam woke and wailed from his basket. I am sitting now with him in the rocking chair on the deck. The afternoon sun is warm on my face and brilliant on the water of the channel. A freighter is passing north along the Saltspring side, heading for Chemainus or Ladysmith to pick up a load of raw logs for Taiwan, Japan or Russia. Normally, Liam would turn his head at the pulsing rumble of the engines. But he is nursing, hungry gulps of air and milk. We call him the guzzler. He is desperate for the thin stream of bluish liquid, all he has ever eaten in his three short months of life. He is comical; ten enormous sucks of milk, then he spits out the nipple and pants like a marathon runner. He gropes wildly for the nipple again; his little fists knead against my skin like a kitten. It makes me laugh. I think he does it on purpose, for my amusement.

I wish I felt like laughing, but Peter's lament bothers me. *I don't know what you are thinking.* I had always thought of us as the perfect couple, in tune, of one mind. It hurts to hear I alone am a blank page to him.

I wonder if I will be a blank page to this little one in my lap. Or will he sense sadness behind my laughter? Will he phone me from halfway around the world because he knows I am sick? Will we both start speaking the same words at the same time? Will we fly like the eagles in unison from our perches? I can't imagine anything else at this moment. Mother and son. We spend hours rocking and nursing like this together. It's different when people meet as adults. This one will know me for every moment of his life. I was his first sight, first smell, first touch. Months of floating in my womb listening to my heartbeat and the sound of my voice. Except for one tiny sperm, he is made entirely of me. Surely, we will know much more than merely each other's thoughts.

103

I must start dinner; the sun is low in the western sky. I have to admit something else bothers me about Peter's comment. I have been sitting here trying to imagine if I knew what Peter was thinking while we cleared broom. You know, I don't have a clue.

EIGHT

For the next two days, Maggie avoided the garden where
Alan worked. She tried to ignore the clink of his tools and
the thud of rock on earth. Sometimes he would sing. She
felt she should offer him a coffee, a glass of water, but the
thought of speaking to him again was unsettling.

She circled aimlessly through the house. Bedroom,
kitchen, living room, bedroom . . . unsure of what she was
seeking. Another drawing, another glimpse of a familiar figure at the desk or gazing out the living room window. Lost
in a maze of memories, she felt the languid weight of
depression, unmotivated to do what she had come for. To
ready the house for its new owners, to scatter Peter's ashes.

She slept late, retired early and napped on a deck chair in
the afternoon. Food didn't interest her. For the sake of
directed activity she prepared toast and coffee upon waking
and opened a can of soup after dark, which she ate with a
few crackers by the light of a kerosene mantle lamp.

On the fourth day, she wandered the northeast side of

the island along the ridge and down to the reef. Everything on the island was familiar. She knew each bush, each turn in every trail, the view over the channel from any point along the way. The trees had grown. An arbutus seedling that sprouted the year Liam was born now stood taller than she could reach. Other trees had fallen. One big fir was uprooted on its side, the roots resting on the cliff top, the broken crown in the sea.

When she reached the beach, she kicked off her shoes and socks and waded through the frigid water. The shell bottom shone white through the clear shallows, abrasive on her feet. Maggie liked to think she and Peter were the first humans to inhabit the island, but she knew it wasn't true. Other women had waded barefoot through this same water to dump baskets of clam shells centuries ago. Along the eroded shoreline, layers of decomposing shell mingled with rich, black soil. If she dug into the crumbling compost, she might be lucky to find bits of pottery, arrowheads and stone tools, the only evidence of the families who stopped for a few days to collect shellfish from the pockets of sand along the shoreline. Ancient middens like this one littered the Gulf Islands, some metres deep and holding fragments of longhouses, human bones in ceremonial graves, evidence of human habitation back five thousand years. Thousands of years. If she stood motionless on a windless day, she might hear the faint murmur of women singing as they worked.

She picked up a mussel shell. The curved interior was a striking blue and the holdfast intact. It would be perfect for a basket. But her tools were all in town. She had no workshop. If she scattered Peter's ashes, the basket making was finished. She dropped the shell back onto the beach and wandered along the tide line.

The retreating tide had deposited broad bands of sea let‐
tuce on the sand and rocks. She crouched and picked up a
piece, the thin seaweed slippery and cold in her hand. The
frond was folded in half, the two sides pasted together with
seawater and slime. Gently, she pulled the halves apart. The
frond tore down the middle and she tossed the fragments
into the water. It had been foolish to think this flimsy plant
was suitable for a basket. It was far too thin. She gathered
another piece, pulled it smooth, then doubled it again. She
pondered the glistening emerald green sheet and thought of
the basket in the back of the car. Perhaps two layers would
give the sea lettuce sufficient strength to prevent cracking.
She held it up; the sun filtered through in patches of light
and dark. Draping several of the fragile plants across her
palm, she carried them back to the house and left them in a
bucket of water on the deck to soak.

The next day Maggie paddled the canoe along the shore‐
line of Galiano, searching for seals and otters. The sun was
warm. She pulled the canoe up on a rocky ledge, secured its
bowline to a driftwood log and curled up inside one of the
sandstone caves. It reminded her of a womb, the smooth
grainy walls curved around her. What would it be like to be
a foetus again, floating warm and safe inside her own moth‐
er's womb? Her life bright and beckoning; the first breath
yet untaken. She longed to rewrite her life and leave out all
the sad stories, all the grief and loneliness. She would keep
the good parts—Peter, the children, their life on the island.
Maybe she would even make kelp baskets, but not for ashes.
She would make them for the pleasure of it, for herself.

She awoke an hour later to find the tide had risen, water
splashing over the lip of the cave. Her jeans were wet with
seawater, the canoe afloat and banging rhythmically against
a rock. On the way back to the island she stopped at the car

107

to collect another pair of jeans and a few tins of soup. When she spied the basket in the bag on the back seat, she thought of the bucket of sea lettuce on the porch. She put the basket in with the food. Perhaps it could occupy a few hours of her evening.

After dinner Maggie laid out the wet algae from the porch in the mudroom to dry a little and brought the basket to the kitchen table. Idly turning it over and over in the lamplight, she wished for inspiration. Maybe mussel shells would look nice, or periwinkles. Perhaps if she inverted the kelp form, it would be easier to lay the sheets. Maybe if it dried slowly in the cool of the mudroom, it wouldn't crack. She crumbled the remaining seaweed clinging to the kelp frame onto the table.

Maggie looked out the window. All she could see in the darkness was her own reflection; her face blurred in the glass and the cast of the lamplight. How could she concentrate when the mood in the house was as unsteady as her own reflected image? She walked restlessly through the rooms, surprised at the aura of apprehension in the air. In Vancouver, her home had been saturated with grief. There she felt emptiness, an absence of life, the notion of fullness drained. But the island house seemed alive, animate, with a throbbing heart and a voice that spoke to her of things she would not hear, reminded her of things best forgotten.

She longed for the simplicity of her car, the cozy nest she had created, the narrow, enclosed space that both contained and protected her. Here the high vaulted ceilings, the walls of windows and the skylights provided too much space, gave too much potential for thought and filled too easily with unanswered whispers in the night.

She put the basket away on a shelf in the kitchen and undressed, climbing onto the high bed in the windowed alcove. She had once been certain she would live out her days here. Remnants of that past clarity lingered in her, broken shards of a powerful love, a love she had not felt before or since. Peter had once accused her of loving the house more than she loved him. In the heat of that argument, she had been tempted to agree with him. He could be so damn obtuse.

Mytilus edulis
BLUE MUSSEL

Peter is mad—off his rocker, out of his mind, crazy as a loony bird. I'm mad too. But the other kind. Pissed off, furious, wild, angry. I wonder if he is sick. What other explanation could there be?

This afternoon, I was kneading a batch of bread. The children were sprawled on big pillows in the living room playing an invented game with strings of blue mussel shells. Liam's skinny legs seemed to take over the floor. Soon he'll be a teenager. Joy has always been a bit chubby, but healthy, nut brown from hours on the beach. What a fish that one is. Not dry a minute all summer.

Today the air held the scent of fall. A heavy layer of fog hung like a thick curtain across the channel. Days like this are comforting, like the weight of a quilt on a cold night. Even the foghorn at Porlier Pass is soothing, its long two-note song easing through the fog every ten minutes.

The room was cozy, permeated with the fragrance of the first warm loaves, fresh from the wood-fired oven. Outside, the leaves of the Garry oaks were starting to change colour and drop off, the gnarled branches twisting up through the white mist until they disappeared. Early this morning the kids made their first leaf pile, jumping and hiding in the crunchy caramel-brown heaps. On a clear day, across the channel on Saltspring, the gold of maples and alders blazes like fire among the evergreens.

I love the fall. Summer is busy with the garden, beach afternoons, too many parties on Galiano. When the days become shorter and the mornings crisp, it feels right to withdraw inside, like spinning a cocoon. All of us get more introspective. The children are content to curl up with a book in front of the wood stove. They feel more like doing their schoolwork. I thought home schooling would be harder. But they thrive on it. Liam said today he would like to do a project on the sea birds that come here in the winter. Where they come from. Why they come here. They are arriving now. I saw a few pigeon guillemots down in the cove yesterday. I can give him my old camera. Joy's a bit of an artist like her father. The kitchen walls are covered with her paintings and stories. I hate to think we might have to leave here for a few years when they are old enough for high school, but it's probably best. Teenagers need more than their family.

I couldn't have imagined a more idyllic day. There I was with my hands in the sticky bread dough, flour down my shirt, when Peter walked in and changed it all. I thought he was angry with me for not helping haul firewood from Galiano. It's an all-day job. Each log goes into the back of the pickup, into the wheelbarrow, into the boat, from the boat to the wheelbarrow, the wheelbarrow to the trailer, up the hill and into the woodshed. I get tired thinking about it. But the bread couldn't wait and the children had been begging me for cinnamon rolls for weeks.

I heard the tractor coming up the hill. Peter appeared at the door and sat down at the kitchen table. The mood in the house shifted. The kids jumped up, the shells clattering onto the floor from their laps, and ran over to him as they always did. When they saw his face, they stopped in mid-step.

I offered him a thick slice of warm bread slathered in butter and honey to cheer him up—a peace offering.

He covered his face with his hands and said, "I've ruined it."

"What, the tractor?" I guessed. Had he had an accident?

"No, the island. I've ruined it."

"What do you mean?" I said. "How does one ruin an island in one afternoon?"

"By building here, I've ruined it." He groaned. "It was pristine when Granddad had it. I remember coming here with him when I was little. I had never been anywhere so wild and amazing. I'd pretend I was an animal, like a raccoon, or a deer that swam over here. I'd make little burrows in the woods and hide stashes of food in secret places, like the kids do. I knew I'd always be safe here. Now there's a trail—no, not a trail—a goddamn road, a tractor, outhouses, solar panels and this great hulk of a house. I've taken paradise and wrecked it."

"You must be tired." I searched for something to say. "I know it's too much. Going back and forth to Vancouver to teach art classes and keeping up with your freelancing. Maybe I can work. Maybe the school would hire me. The kids wouldn't mind going to school." I turned to them. "Would you, kids?"

They had moved together, Joy leaning back against Liam, his hands protectively on her shoulders. They nodded dumbly, eyes wide.

"I could help with the mortgage. Hey, I know. We could

113

finish the room below the deck and rent to tourists. Paula told me—"

"Mags. You don't get it. It's not the work. Or the money. Everywhere I turn, I see the mess I've made of it. We should never have built here . . . I want to sell."

I couldn't believe he was saying this in front of the children. He might as well have told us he wanted a divorce. I felt a lump, heavy as the dough I had been kneading, form in my gut. He couldn't mean it. We were meant to grow old here. I couldn't leave this place. How could this be creation to me and destruction to him?

"We can talk about this later," I said, punching my fists into the fleshy dough to keep myself from yelling at him.

My jaw ached with tension. How could he conclude we had ruined this island? Ruined! What about all the things we didn't do? No power poles, no barges, no wood preservative, no excavation, no septic field. We'd been careful, so careful, talking over every little decision. We hadn't cut down a single tree. We brought our firewood here in a rowboat, for God's sake.

I don't know what possessed me. I wanted to shut him up. I wanted to hurt him. I pulled a sticky wad of dough out of the mound, stretched my arm behind my head and threw the wad across the room. He ducked and put his hand up to shield his face. The dough hit him on the wrist, clinging to the edge of his sleeve for a moment before falling to the floor. Joy giggled. Peter took a step toward me but I wasn't going to give him the satisfaction of retaliation. I stepped forward in front of him, crossed my arms and said, in a low hiss I hoped the children couldn't hear, "Well, burn it down then."

His face flushed red, his eyelids narrowed and after a moment he said through clenched teeth, "I might do that. It seems you love this house more than you love me."

He was gone, slamming the door. The tractor started up and we listened to the rattle of the diesel engine fade towards the water. Inside, the children and I stood in a circle watching the lump of dough flatten and spread across the floor.

NINE

The full moon hung like an enormous silver dish over the Saltspring Island hills, reflecting light across the channel and into the room. Peter sat naked by the window at the foot of the bed as though he had been there for a long time. He had always slept naked, even on the coldest nights of winter when Maggie would wrap herself in layers of flannel.

He reached out and she gathered his hand into hers. She was afraid—afraid her fingers would pass through his—and was surprised at the feel of solid flesh against solid flesh. With his free hand, Peter gestured toward the moonlit channel. An eerie tone like the low of a saxophone sounded from a distance. In the shining circle cast mid-channel by the moon, she could make out shapes in motion. She turned to Peter and he smiled, his eyes midnight blue in the diffuse glow. She looked again to the sea. A large dorsal fin sliced through the silver orb, two more and another three. *Orcinus orca*, killer whales.

In unison, a pair breached from the water, their giant

bulks suspended momentarily in mid-air before crashing down in a surge of sea spray. Others slapped the water with their massive tails, or thrust their heads inquisitively into the air to look around. Then they disappeared, spiralling down to emerge several body lengths away, mist spouting from each blowhole. As they played, the whales sang an unearthly song. The music skimmed across the ocean surface and flooded the house with its melody.

She did not know how long they sat together watching the spectacle. Peter's arms around her, her hand in his, neither daring to breathe. Maggie felt humbled by the ballet performed for their eyes only.

Then Peter's lips were on her neck, her shoulder, the hollow in her throat. She turned into him and they made love, the keen of the whales mingling with their own sounds, their bodies bathed in the lunar brilliance.

Maggie awoke to her own cry, her hands between her thighs. The dawn was near and the world colourless in the prelight of those early hours. The whales were gone, were they ever there? Yes, there had been a night like it years ago . . . and Peter? Maggie slipped out of bed and, in her bathrobe, padded through the house, peering into every room. She walked onto the bedroom deck and shivered in the morning chill. She was alone.

Off to the southeast, wild charcoal clouds were forming in the brightening sky. She could feel the pressure of Peter's hands on her skin in the night. She rubbed her fingers along her arm to brush away the sensation.

Sounds below the deck drew her to the glass and cedar railing where she had an unobstructed view of the garden, the meadow and the oak and arbutus grove. Alan Page was already at work on the rock staircase. He was shirtless in spite of the cold and beads of sweat had risen on his back. He struggled to shift a large slab of sandstone into place. Maggie thought he looked too old for this hard physical work, hauling heavy stones up and down steep slopes. His dark hair was peppered with grey and white; he must be at least fifty. He stood, arched his back and rolled his head from shoulder to shoulder. Maggie stepped away from the railing.

"Hello!" he yelled.

She cursed under her breath and moved forward to nod over the railing at him.

"Sorry if I woke you. I wanted to get a bit done before it rains," he said.

Across the channel, Saltspring Island was already swathed in cloud and sheets of misty rain obscured the shoreline. Alan took a large, checkered bandanna from his pocket and wiped the sweat from his face. He looked up at her. Conscious she was dressed only in a bathrobe, Maggie fumbled for a reason to flee.

"You'll have to excuse me," she said. "I have to ... get a pot from the stove."

Before she could retreat, Alan called, "Would you mind if I had a glass of water?"

Maggie nodded, embarrassed by her thoughtlessness. "Yes, of course."

When she returned with a jug of water and a glass, he was already up on the deck, leaning against the railing, gazing down the channel where bright fingers of the rising sun were creeping through the trees. She handed the glass to him and he drank deeply, his head thrown back, neck rippling with the passage of the water down his throat. Maggie turned her eyes from the fine, dark curl of hair on his chest. Her cheeks warmed at the memory of her dream. To deflect the rush of colour that must have passed across her face, to remind herself this man was not Peter, she spoke to him.

"That looks like hard work."

"Yeah, it is," he said, holding out the glass for a refill. "But us old guys know how to conserve energy. Brains, not brawn, they say. The young guys heave them into place. I haven't hurt myself yet."

He took another mouthful of water. "I was sorry to hear about your husband."

The words were unexpected; she had to fight to check the bite of tears. "I—well, that was a while ago."

"Doesn't matter. I lost a daughter seven years ago and I still miss her like hell."

"Oh." Maggie searched for words to reply but could only mumble, "I'm sorry."

"Me too, but in a twisted way it was a blessing. Brought me to the island. I came here for respite from the memories for a couple of weeks. Never left, except to close up my office and sell my house. I even joined the volunteer fire department." He winked. "I should be able to call myself an islander in a decade or so." He gestured toward the house. "You have a fine place here. I was an architect. This house is a bit of genius. I wish I had designed it. But that's in the past. I just build rock walls now. It's more therapy than anything. You can hammer on sandstone all you want and it doesn't argue back. And I get to be outside."

He handed her the glass. "Well, thanks for the water. I'd better get back to work, let out a few more frustrations."

Maggie stood in the doorway and watched Alan thunder down the wooden steps to the garden and pick up his gloves. Getting on with life. The world was full of people like him. Who took the bad, turned it around and carried on.

The rain began just after nine. Maggie sat at the kitchen table drinking yesterday's black coffee, her body drained and tired. Whitecaps stretched up and down the channel. Not a boat was in sight. Alan left when the rain turned heavy, waving at her through the window, the hood of his raincoat thrown over his head. Maggie abandoned her plans to paddle across the channel to the Secretary Islands. Her conversation with Alan, the way he spoke about his daughter, made her think about her own children. Joy's absence. Liam's expectations. This was the sixth day and she was further from fulfilling Liam's orders than she had been sleeping in her car. What would he say if she returned to Vancouver with nothing accomplished, the basket of ashes tucked under her arm? He would have her committed. One step. All she had to do was take one step. The house had sold and even if nothing else, she had to deal with their personal belongings. One item at a time.

She rinsed out her coffee cup. It would be simple—a few pieces of furniture, a couple of paintings, the odd knick-knack. The children would want them. It shouldn't take long.

She began with the footstool in the bathroom. Peter built it for Joy when she was three, so she could reach the bathroom sink. He had whipped it up in a couple of hours out of plywood. He and Joy had painted it together—black and white bunnies in a meadow, a tree loaded with red apple blobs, a nest of chicks, a bright yellow sun and fluffy clouds. Joy used it every day until she was ten, years after she could reach the sink unaided. Maggie wrote "Joy" on a sticker and stuck it over a bunny ear.

She lifted a canvas off the kitchen wall. It was an island landscape by a local artist. An acrylic scene of the cove. It had been a surprise for one of Peter's birthdays. Maggie ran her hand across it and smiled. He had admired it in the local co-op gallery. On the day of his birthday, while on their Friday excursion to Sturdies Bay for supplies, she concocted an excuse and slipped away. She drove to the gallery and purchased the painting. Then sped breakneck to the cove, rowed over to the island and ran up the path, the painting banging against her leg. She hung it in the kitchen where he couldn't miss seeing it. When she arrived back at the village an hour later, Peter was absorbed in conversation with Caleb Leighman, the postman. Liam, his face smeared with chocolate ice cream, was balanced on Peter's shoulders. When they arrived home, Peter walked into the kitchen and almost dropped his armload of groceries. The expression on his face was precious. He stood, dumbstruck at the sight of the painting, looking back and forth from Maggie to the painting like he had seen a miracle.

Maggie brushed a layer of dust from the frame and turned it over. "For Liam" she wrote in pencil on the cardboard backing.

As she moved about the house, labelling each piece with a name and directions for the movers, the air became dense with memories of her life with Peter and the children. By late afternoon, the rain had not eased. She usually found the gentle drumming of raindrops on the roof and skylights, and the moaning of the wind through the treetops outside, soothing, but today she grew increasingly edgy.

Only one item was left to label, a large antique cabinet in the living room. Peter had converted the old European wardrobe into a cupboard where he kept his art supplies. It stood taller than Peter, imposing. Darkened with age, the ancient oak smelled faintly of rancid oil and beeswax. The front door was inlaid with mahogany and the top edges carved with a twisting grapevine. The year "1785" was inscribed on the lintel. She suspected it was valuable. It was heavy and awkward, and they had left it on the island when they moved to Vancouver.

Maggie turned the hand-hewn iron key in the lock and swung open the heavy door. She felt wicked, for Peter had never let anyone open it. Including her. It was his secret chest of wonders. She had often seen the children, especially Joy, peering through the thin crack in the door, aching to glimpse her father's forbidden treasures. Maggie had been tempted to open the cupboard during those long nights when Peter was in Vancouver teaching. As far as she knew, this was the single secret Peter had ever kept from her. They had petty arguments about it; she called him juvenile, he accused her of disrespect. Maggie chuckled when she noticed the spot near the bottom of the door where Joy had carved her name and a picture of a cat with a red pencil. Peter was furious and Joy jubilant, in spite of the scolding, at her revenge for her father's secrecy. Now the shelves were empty except for a light skim of dust and a few dead flies. It was going to be hard to move; Peter had a complicated method for dismantling it. Maggie didn't have a clue how to do it. Peter wasn't here to help her. She stared at the bare shelves.

"Not here," she whispered.

Not here. The words echoed around the inside of the open cupboard and into the room. They pulled an injured cry from Maggie's throat. She was overwhelmed by a fury that contracted every muscle in her body. With both hands, she grasped the edge of the heavy door and, using the force of her being, slammed it shut. The entire structure shook; the noise reverberated through the empty house.

"You're not here now. And you weren't here then!" she shouted, her fists beating on the unyielding wooden surface. "Goddamnit, you weren't here!"

She raised her knee to her chest and kicked her leg against the cabinet. She ran from the house to the wood-pile. Wrenching the large splitting axe from the big cedar chopping block, she dragged it behind her and charged back through the house. She stood in front of the cupboard, chest heaving, then lifted the axe with both hands above her shoulder. It swung awkwardly against the solid cupboard door. The ancient timber resisted. The blade glanced off the hard surface and the impact threw her off balance. She staggered against the wall, her shoulder twisting with the weight of the axe. She lifted it again, her feet spread for stability, and struck for a second time. She had a notion she was crying, or screaming, but her focus was on the dark grain of the wood. This time, the axe blade sliced into the door. She pulled it out with difficulty and swung again. The door splintered. With each swing, she screamed the same words, "Not here! Not here! Not here!"

The metal axe head left gaping pale wounds of newly exposed wood. Jagged splinters twisted from the frame and fell, crackling like close thunder. The frame yielded bit by bit. The door tore squealing from the iron hinges. The heavy top crashed down in one piece; the walls collapsed inward. Maggie pulled the back down with her bare hands. She continued her assault with weapon and flesh until the cabinet was unrecognizable. Panting and dazed, she waded through the wreckage, letting the axe drop from her hand, then ran from the house.

Nereocystis luetkeana
BULL KELP

I have been to heaven and hell in one night.

Yesterday, yesterday seems so long ago. Yesterday there was a storm.

A late winter storm blew up in the afternoon from the southwest. Winds from the southwest are the worst for the cove. They blow in through the narrow gap between the two islands and the breaking waves heave onto the beach, broadsiding any small craft that tries to make the crossing.

I knew by five o'clock Peter would not get home. He had been away for six days, working in Vancouver. The editor of the textbook he is illustrating called last week in a panic about deadlines and he went, just like that. He goes to Vancouver more and more these days. Especially now he's teaching at both Emily Carr and Langara College. I'm glad at his success. And of course we need the money. I'm so damn supportive, but I wish he hadn't gone, not now. He knew I was due in six weeks. But I didn't want him to think

I couldn't manage. I assured him three-year-old Liam would do a good job of looking after me.

Liam loved to sit in what was left of my lap, his golden curls pressed against my swollen tummy, listening, jumping up in excitement when he felt the kick of a miniature foot or the roll of a tiny bum across my drum-tight skin. I told Peter that Paula was simply a call away on the marine radio. I didn't tell him Paula was furious at him for leaving me pregnant, alone with Liam, on the island.

By the time I had Liam in bed, stories read, kissed and cuddled, the wind was howling. Branches from overhanging trees scraped across the cedar shake roof. I could see, in the dimming light, large breakers on the channel, the tops of the waves blowing off into gusts of white spray—more than twenty knots by the Beaufort scale. No ferry tonight. I lit the tall kerosene lantern on the kitchen table and another by the bed and carried one over to the shelf where we kept the marine radio.

I thought I'd give Paula a call to see if she'd heard anything. When I turned on the radio, there was no response. I wasn't worried. The swaying branches might have caught the wires between the solar panel on the roof and the batteries that supplied us with power to run the radio and a few lights. No big deal. Easy to fix the next day.

But I was wrong, nothing will be easy to fix after last night.

As I stood by the radio in the wavering shadow of the lamp, the transmitter in my hand, I heard the faint, curious sound of water dripping. Dampness seeped into my wool socks. I looked up at the ceiling for a leak. Nothing but dry cedar panelling. I looked down. Water ran from beneath my long skirt and pooled onto the floor. My thighs were drenched in a flood of warm fluid. It ran from me like an

endless waterfall from an infinite lake. I stood transfixed by
the sensation of formlessness in my pelvis. The bottom of
my soul had dissolved; I was swirling into an abyss. As the
last tepid drops trickled from me, I knew. My water had
broken. My time had come and I was alone.

Panic welled in my chest. I flicked the radio off and on
again, struggling to hold the transmitter in my shaking
hands.

"Vancouver Coastguard Radio, Vancouver Coastguard
Radio—this is the Islander. The Islander."

Nothing. Goddamnit, nothing.

The first contraction dropped me to my knees, and I
crouched in the now cold amniotic fluid. I fought to
breathe as the spasm rolled over and down my body. The
wind of the storm outside breached the walls of the house
and penetrated through the pores of my skin, howling in a
tempest through me from head to toe. After the contraction
had passed, I lay on the floor for a moment, eyes closed,
fighting to suppress the scream that rose in my throat. I
thought of the broken radio, the storm raging outside, the
dark, dark night. Peter . . . he might as well be a million
miles away. And the sleeping boy upstairs. Liam, who pat-
ted my cheek as I tucked him into bed and said, "I take care
of you, Mama, you and baby."

I pushed myself up and hobbled to the sink for a tea
towel, then knelt to wipe up the lake of fluid. The second
contraction hit. It couldn't have been five minutes since the
last one. It was too fast. Too early. "Not now, little one," I
prayed. I crawled to the bed, but I was unable to climb up
on my own. I pulled the quilt onto the floor.

Time dissolved. Contractions crashed upon me like
waves upon the rocks of the island. I was grateful for the
light of the kerosene lamp at the bedside and I prayed it

wouldn't go out. My lips were parched and dry. I managed to stumble to the bathroom for a bit of water, a towel, a pair of scissors and the wastebasket, things a vague, faraway logic told me I might need. I remembered a pouch of powdered herbs—the dried leaves of rattlesnake plantain— Paula had given me, to ease the pain when it's time, she had said. I drew the embroidered cotton pouch from the drawer on my desk and shook the powder into the water glass. The fine brown particles floated like a skim of pondweed on the surface. I drank.

Time turned inside out. A minute felt like hours, hours like seconds. I found myself floating against the bedroom ceiling, watching a woman writhe on a quilt on the floor. Her face, I didn't recognize her face, eyes bulging with effort, her teeth sunken into the wooden leg of a chair to muffle her cries. I wanted to help her, but I couldn't get myself down. I was too tired.

I became that woman, my face hers, twisted and grim, wood grain between my teeth so my son wouldn't hear. I could endure the pain and exhaustion no more. I lapped the dry herbs from the bag like a starving animal. I gagged on the earthy texture and was close to vomiting when the urge to push gripped me. It was like no other feeling, like an external command from afar. A deep growl escaped my throat; every cell of my body vibrated with its depth. It was both terrifying and wondrous, for I could no sooner stop it than I could stop a tornado—nor did I want to. When it passed, I reached between my legs and felt the sticky down of the head. I cupped my palm around the top of the skull. It barely filled my hand.

I tried to remember what I had read about premature babies. Could a six-week premie survive without an incubator? I wasn't prepared. I didn't even have any diapers. Paula was going to bring me bull kelp. To heat and drape on my stomach. She said it was an old native remedy. To make the child as slippery as seaweed, to ease the passage. But it wasn't needed. Two more pushes and the baby slid from me. Slippery enough; blood and strings of mucous gushed out around it.

I sat back onto my heels and gathered the wet, vernix-coated body into my arms. I tucked the towel around us for warmth. The fire was cold in the stove.

I drew the cloth back from the tiny part of me that had slipped from my uterus. It was a girl. I wiped the mucous from her rosette mouth. She was limp and motionless, her skin tinged with blue. I clamped my mouth over her face, sucking to pull the birth slime from her throat. She mewed once like a kitten, then her delicate chest moved, her skin gained colour. A final contraction and the placenta spilled onto the floor between my legs. I lay back, holding her, rocking us both—powerful, terrified, jubilant, helpless.

"Mama, is you okay?" Liam stood at the door to the bedroom, his drowsy eyes taking in the sight of the room—his naked, tear-stained mother, the bloody quilt, the quivering placenta, the towel bundled in my arms. My mind churned frantically for words. I could send him back to bed. He would think it was a dream. Instinct pulled me from the lie.

"Yes, sweetie. It's time. She's come."

I beckoned him. He tiptoed toward us. The smile that splashed across his face drove the rage of the storm and the past infinite hours from me.

He stood beside us, eyes only for his sister. "Can me hold her?" he asked.

I sat him on the floor and showed him how to keep her head from falling back. Carefully, he overlapped his arms and received her weight. He began to sing his favourite lullaby. "Hush a ba, don you cwy, go to sweep you liddle ba-bee."

I reached for the scissors and cut a narrow strip of cloth from the edge of the towel. My fingers could detect no pulse in the sinewy umbilical cord. Tying a clumsy knot around the twisted vein, I snipped the placenta free. The quivering mass slid into the wicker wastebasket. I heaved myself up and shuffled to the bathroom to wash the blood from my body. The warm water felt good on my skin.

Liam's sweet voice wafted through the house. "Hush a ba, don you cwy, all la pweddy liddle hoases."

I put on a clean nightgown and a pad to gather the blood that would flow from me for the days to come. An old flannel baby blanket of Liam's in my hand, I stood in the bedroom doorway for a moment, watching him. His hair wild and tangled with the restless sleep of a child, his head bent, intent on the important job he was charged with.

"Bwacks 'n bays, dappos 'n gways, all you pweddy liddle hoases."

With the help of a chair, we climbed into the bed and I pulled the bloody quilt over us, a child cradled in each arm. Exhausted, I swaddled the baby in the flannel blanket against my breast. Liam couldn't resist the urge to touch her. He reached across me and tugged away the covers to massage her back in gentle circles with his chubby fingers. She looked so fragile, her skin translucent, her fingers and toes thin as spider legs. I pulled my nipple to her lips and slid my finger through her mouth. Nothing. She was too weak to suck. Liam worriedly watched my futile efforts. How could I tell him? I did not know what the words would be until I heard myself speak.

"Liam, Mama needs you to be her brave boy, okay?"

I worked to keep my voice steady. Liam nodded, his eyes shone.

"The baby's only here for a short visit. To say hi. So you know who she is. Then she has to go away."

"Like Daddy?"

"No, honey. Forever. She has a job to do. She's going to be an angel."

"Oh," he said.

He leaned over me and kissed her. Her eyes opened, clear and blue and wise. She looked at her brother in recognition. Their eyes locked together. For an instant, a bond of perfect love hovered between them. Her eyelids slid to her cheeks, the long black lashes settling feather-light onto her tender skin. A gentle sigh escaped her lips and she was quiet. A stream of transparent white vapour spiralled upward from the crown of her downy head and dissipated. Liam was watching it too, following it with his eyes, up, up to the ceiling. Even after the mist had vanished, his gaze lingered.

"Mama, can we name her Angel?"

"Yes, honey, we can."

Outside the light of the dawn was streaming across the now peaceful channel.

Peter found us this morning. He must have paused at the top of the stairs, marvelling at the tender scene, mother and son cuddled together, the morning sun streaming across the bed. Outside, the silence after the storm. Liam's white-gold curls glowing in the light like a halo. Peter might have noticed other things: the stained quilt, the wastebasket of dark purple organ, the marks on the desk. Or perhaps they did not register, so intent was he on the idyllic scene. He must have tiptoed across the room, trying not to wake us, and bent to brush his lips against the forehead of his sleeping son. He would have seen the tiny bundle of flannel tucked between us, the smooth cap of fine hair. I woke to hear his soft "Oh God," and watched him touch the stiff, blue miniature fingers wrapped around Liam's thumb.

I was surprised to read no guilt in his eyes.

TEN

The ground welcomed her. The cushion of moss accepted her tears and wicked them downwards where they were forgotten. Maggie struggled for a moment against this unexpected embrace of earth and vegetation. She beat her fists upon the spongy, green carpet of moss; each blow was absorbed into the forest floor until, spent, she quieted.

Maggie rolled over and opened her eyes. Her arms and legs were scratched and bleeding from her wild run from the house. Daylight had softened towards dusk. The air, heavy with the smell of decay, was damp and cool from the day's rain and the impending night. A bat flitted through the canopy of boughs overhead. Here on the north corner of the island, the forest was close and dark. It was old forest; it had never been logged. On the other side where the island was open to the sea, the trees were bent and aged like wizened people twisting against the prevailing winds. But here they rose tall and straight with huge, furrowed trunks rising thirty metres or more into the sky. This was where the eagles had their nest—which tree, she could not be sure.

Little sunlight found its way through the dense canopy. The forest floor was open; only a few brave seedlings had managed to sprout in the shadow of the giants. Dark-loving plants proliferated; thick mats of moss, sword fern and chin-high banks of straggly salal were strewn with limbs of dead trees rotting on the ground. Maggie imagined herself one of them—gnarled, withered, open to the insects, the weather—soon to be transformed.

This place was familiar. Surely she had walked here at least once during her years on the island, although she had most often sought out the warm sun of the cliffside. The children may have made a fort between the firs or in the hollow where the roots of a fallen tree had been ripped from the ground during a storm. She searched for a worn telltale rope hanging from a branch or a piece of broken tea set in the ferns, but there was nothing. Here it was pure, untainted for all time by humans. It didn't matter; from this moment on, this place would be a monument, her burial mound, her graveyard.

She closed her eyes to imprint the details of it on her memory—in case there would be memory in death. As she imagined the landscape in her mind, she knew. She had seen this grove of fir and moss described in pen and ink in detail on a single sheet of drawing paper. The simple sheet of paper on Peter's table in the bedroom. She wondered if her body had now been sketched into the drawing, or if she had already decomposed, the scene identical before and after, save for a few insignificant piles of added humus that had once been a woman. Peter had drawn her here and she had come. *Take me to the forest.*

How much time would it require, this death and decomposition? It might be quick. A night in the open, exposed to

134

air and moisture, the cold and damp seeping into her, immobilizing her until she slept, deeply, not to waken. One short night . . . or two. She would be lucky if that were so.

Or it would take a long time, days to lose consciousness from lack of water and food, weeks for the flesh to fall to decomposers and scavengers. They would come with silent feet on hidden trails in the night—the insects, the rodents—or noisily by day—the crows and seagulls, and the eagles. Would she be aware of their nibbling? The piercing of their claws and teeth and beaks? Would she feel them take her apart, bit by bit, until a talon would snap the line that held her to life?

What would happen after that? Would her soul hover above her, keeping vigil in the years her bones lay undiscovered? Or would there be only darkness?

She was so cold.

Collinsia parviflora
BLUE-EYED MARY

The fire has been burning a day and a half. I think it must be enough time, but I'm not sure. I throw more branches on the pile and the dry leaves clinging to the wood sizzle and flash into flame. There is not much smoke; the fire is too hot. That is good. It has to be very, very hot.

Liam is asleep behind me on the sleeping bag next to the fire where we spent the night. Peter gave in and brought the bag to us with extra blankets and mugs of hot soup. The flames of the fire kept the March chill at bay. I think I can see the edges of the tin box among the coals, the paint blackened and curling, the train chugging across the metallic landscape no longer visible. Inside, I imagine the body of Angel, dissolving to dust and ash.

I am so tired, I don't know if I can walk to the house. I have been using moss to soak up the blood that trickles from my spent womb. I toss the used moss into the flames. I guess I would throw myself in too if I didn't have Liam. Peter doesn't understand. Yesterday morning when he found us, he went straight for the marine radio.

"I'll call Dr. Grant and we'll get you to the hospital," he proclaimed.

Thank God, the radio was broken. I hadn't felt thankful last night, but now I was glad.

"No!" I shouted. I slid off the bed.

Peter turned to watch me grimace. "What did you say?"

"No," I repeated. "I'm fine. Peter, I want to cremate her . . . here. The three of us. I don't want anyone else here."

He opened his mouth to speak, his face pale against his red fleece jacket, and closed it without a word. He started pacing. He does that when he is confronted with a problem. Pacing to stir up a solution out of the air as he strides round and round on his long legs.

"The problem, Maggie," he urged—he thinks I am losing my mind—"is that we need to let people know. We can't do this ourselves. It's . . . it must be illegal."

"They'll take her away. She needs to stay here. She's only a newborn." I stood, planted between Peter and the radio. I was weak, swaying like the trunk of a hundred-year-old fir in a gale-force wind.

"But what will people say? One day you're pregnant, the next you're not?" He was waving his arms, exasperated.

"I don't care what people say. People on the island say all kinds of things. Besides, once they hear I had a miscarriage they won't ask any more questions," I said. "People don't like talking about things like miscarriages. They'll make their own assumptions, gossip about what they want, and leave us alone. I'm going outside to build the fire."

I guess he sensed truth in what I said because he let me go without another word. I hobbled from the bedroom to the path that led around the house to the meadow. Liam, dressed in his teddy bear pajamas, had been listening attentively from the bed, Angel swaddled in the flannel blanket next to him. He followed me.

"Mama," he called from the deck, his voice desperate. "Me come too."

Of course, I remembered, he had always been afraid of my leaving him. I went back and knelt, placing my hands on his shoulders. I looked him in the eye.

139

"Would you like to help me, Liam?"

He nodded and caressed my face with his trusting fingers.

"Can you find a little box to put Angel in?" I said.

He frowned, thoughtful. His face lit up and he smiled, turned and ran up the stairs to his room. Minutes later he was back, carrying a green and red tin candy box about the size of a shoebox, an old-fashioned train chugging through a winter landscape stencilled on its sides. Once containing Christmas sweets sent from Europe by Peter's uncle, it now held Liam's collection of matchbox cars. He upended the box and miniature dump trucks, police cars, an ambulance and two dozen other vehicles crashed and bounced to the deck. I followed him through the house to the bedroom. Peter was gone. Liam put the box on the bed beside Angel. He hesitated; his gaze shifted between them.

"Can we keep her a few mo' days, Mama?" he said. "Me want to cuddle her for some more."

I gathered him onto my lap. My sweet, sweet son with his dimpled cheeks and his pleading eyes, his sister stiff and hard like a plastic doll. He had seen so much, now knew so much, a three-year-old with the life experience of a grown man. How could I make him let her go when I could not bear the thought myself?

"How about you look after Angel while I build the fire?" I said.

He was happy with that and we settled her into the box.

He tucked the flannel blanket around her face. The playful print—lambs and puffy clouds floating in a sky as blue as Angel's eyes—helped to lighten our sadness.

Together, we went outside to the meadow. I gathered any dry branches and brush I could find, and piled them on a mound of Scotch broom cuttings that had been waiting since last spring to be burned. Liam watched me, proudly clutching the tin box in his arms, chest out, shoulders thrown back, chin up. Soon, he disappeared and returned with the red wooden wagon Peter had built him for his second birthday. Angel in her box bounced along in the back. Liam followed me, stacking twigs around the tin box, diligent in his task. Every so often he would stop and kiss Angel on her nose or forehead, or run his fat fingers over her downy hair.

"She's real cold, mama," he urged. "Can we start the fire now? Me want to warm her up."

Liam and I piled branches higher and higher until the stack was taller than our heads. I had to stop and rest often. I hadn't eaten since before I went into labour. When we were satisfied the pile was ready, we sat side-by-side on a rock with the box. Angel's skin was the colour of the blue-eyed Mary in the meadow. I leaned down and rested my cheek against hers; one warm, one waxy and cold. Liam pulled a plush rabbit from his pocket and laid it beside her, fussing with the edges of the blanket until sister and toy were tightly swaddled. We kissed her and, with one last look, closed the lid.

I pushed the box into the middle of the tangle and, using a long stick, shoved it as far into the centre of the pyre as I could, taking care not to tip it over. The rain from the storm had dampened most of the wood, and it took several tries to get it going. We fed it pieces of kindling that Liam fetched in his wagon from the woodbox in the house. At last, a dry cedar bough caught and the needles flashed into flame, crackling and throwing sparks into the air. We settled onto the ground, holding each other, Liam's head against my shoulder.

"Angel's warm now, isn't she, Mama?" he said.

"Yes, honey, Angel is warm."

He must have felt my tears splash onto the swirl of hair at the crown of his head, but he said nothing more. Peter came, after it was dark, with the sleeping bag and mugs of hot soup. I had expected he wouldn't come and I didn't care. But I was glad when I felt him pull the blanket around us and gather the now-sleeping Liam onto his knee. We sat there in silence, watching the flames lick at the box. To an observer, it would have appeared an innocent family bonfire. But they wouldn't know we were watching the fire consume the body of our daughter.

I am anxious now, waiting for the ash and cinder to cool enough to handle with the garden trowel from the shed. The sun is low in the sky, hanging above the mauve of the Vancouver Island mountains. Pink and gold stain the horizon. The equinox of spring is near. Tonight the sun will set west of the dip that marks its midway run between winter and summer solstice.

Peter stands beside me with a clay bowl, glazed with a pattern of dolphins and birds, ready to receive the remains of his daughter. Liam holds a fistful of early blooming blue-eyed Mary gleaned from the edge of the meadow in one hand and in the other a branch of dwarf rose, scarlet hips tarnished with winter chill, dangling between the fine thorns. He watches the two of us intently and every few minutes asks, "Now, Mama?"

I make sure that I get it all. The coarse pieces of black charcoal, tiny fragments of bone, the thick wood ash that crumbles as I lift it. I am most careful with the fine pearly dust that I imagine holds her tiny fingers and toes, the silent heart, the rosebud lips. There is nothing left of the box except a few teardrops of metal. I take them too, along with a handful of pebbles and the top layer of soil.

I find it hard to walk. The front of my dress is wet with milk. I will have to bind my breasts to discourage the wasted flow. Now I lean on Peter, his arm under my elbow. Liam skips ahead, delighted to be going boating at sunset. Peter rows us out to the middle of the bay. The sun glints off Liam's curls, and, over the Vancouver Island horizon, colours ooze from behind the mountains into the sky as if an unseen artist is squeezing tubes of paint onto a canvas. Liam leans over the bow of the boat, watching for rock crabs through the clear water. I hold the strap of his life-jacket with one hand. The pot of ashes and the bouquet of wildflowers are stowed under my seat. A great blue heron is startled by the splash of the oars and, squawking, lifts off from the eelgrass shallows and glides on soundless stretches of wing into the trees.

"Now, Liam," I say, and he turns to watch me lift the clay pot from the bottom of the boat. He reaches in his chubby hands, already blackened with charcoal from the cold fire, and, laughing, flings fistfuls of ash into the air. The dust drifts down onto the mirror of water, floats suspended for a moment and is gone. Like this we move fluid with the tide the whole length of the cove, Liam laughing and flinging ashes and wildflowers into the water, Peter rowing, the heron watching, the sun sliding down behind the smoky mountains, pink and blue, red and purple swatches taking over the sky. I am crying; my tears follow my daughter down through the frigid water to her bed in the mud at the bottom of the cove.

In the morning, I wake to feel the imprint of a baby in my cradled arms. My whole body curls inwards, searching, to surround her, to pull her back into the safety of my womb. But there is nothing.

143

ELEVEN

"Maggie ..."

She strained to free herself from semi-consciousness. The interminable night had been sleepless; she had descended into a black hole of senselessness where wavering images of mysterious spectres wandered lost through a twisting, muddy maze. Her name, whispered by a familiar voice, had succeeded in reaching her, pulling her from the mire.

She listened for it. The night was filled with sound: the falling call of a nighthawk, the distant croak of frogs on Galiano, above her head the eerie hoot of a barred owl, "Who cooks for youuuu." She must be alive; there can't be barred owls in heaven ... or hell.

"Maggie ..."

"Yes," she murmured.

"If you were to kill yourself, how would you do it?"

"I would lie in the forest until I become earth."

"Maggie."

"Hmmm."

"It doesn't suit you."

Maggie opened her eyes. Peter sat on a log at her feet, eyes full of love, mouth curved in a kind, sad smile. His face was thin, worn and tired, his hair pure white.

Was she already dead? Had he come to collect her? To take her with him?

146 Her body belied the notion of death. It ached. The hills and valleys of the ground pressed into her back. Her fingers and feet were numb to the crush of moss below them. Cold had sifted through her body; she was beyond shivering. Her legs and arms were stiff. Above, dark silhouettes of trees like waiting giants were etched against the moonless, black sky. Groaning with effort, Maggie pushed herself to sitting and drew her knees up to her chest, hugging them not for warmth but for containment.

She stared at him and he stared back. Neither moving, neither speaking. Anger overwhelmed her again.

"It's too late. You've come too late." She hissed the words into the night. "You were always too late. Do you think you can abandon me when Angel was born, abandon me for the last three years, and be here with me now?" she yelled. "Go away!"

Fingers of his breath eased around her, spreading warmth into her pores.

"What do you want?" she asked. "Are you here to watch me die, like I watched you? It that what you want?"

Maggie rested her head on her knees and closed her eyes. She saw herself in the Vancouver house, sitting by Peter's bed. He was asleep. His breath rattled in his lungs with each inhalation and each exhalation. His arm across his chest, wrist cocked in the air. His hand moved in agitated circles, round and round, as if trying to sweep away the pain that found him even in sleep.

Although it was early afternoon, Maggie had drawn the blinds. She sent the children to the store for groceries. They argued with her. Finally, they agreed, reluctant. She knew they sensed the time was near.

A white candle on the bedside table cast shadows on the wall. Maggie held the amber glass bottle of liquid morphine in her lap. She picked up a clean syringe from the tabletop and dipped it into the open mouth of the container. Pulling up the plunger, she drew the clear, odourless syrup into the plastic tube. Her hand steady, she leaned forward and eased the syringe through Peter's lips. With her thumb she squeezed the plunger down to force the fluid in; a small amount dribbled from the corner of his mouth onto the sheet. Maggie wiped it from his chin with a cloth.

She filled the syringe again, the action familiar, habitual; she had done it a hundred times in the past few weeks. She fed him the last of his required dosage, but she didn't stop there. Another syringe and another. Methodically, she filled and squeezed and wiped, one after another. She wasn't sure, was it six now, no, seven? She lost count.

She stopped and waited, watching Peter's face. His hand circled faster and faster in the wavering candlelight, his breath shallow. He muttered silently to himself. Was it enough? Please be quick. As if in response to her prayer, his hand stopped moving. A great long sigh floated out from between his teeth and into the room. The candle flame flickered and went out. She groped his wrist for a pulse. Peter was dead.

She screwed the lid back onto the morphine and placed the bottle on the shelf next to the bed. She washed out the syringe in the bathroom sink and held it to the light to make sure no morphine remained, then dropped it into a plastic cup. Opening the blinds, she climbed onto the bed

beside Peter, her head on his quiet body, the gentle afternoon sun falling across them, and waited for her children.

The owl hooted again at a distance. Maggie opened her
eyes and said, her voice cracking, tears on her cheeks,
"That's it, isn't it, Peter? Don't you know I had to do it?"

Peter shook his head, his eyes pained and forgiving.

"What is it, why are you here? Tell me and leave me in
peace." Maggie stood and stepped toward him, fists
clenched.

Peter held a white cloth bundle up to her. A baby. She
sucked the cold night air into her lungs. *Angel?* Maggie
staggered forward and reached out to pull the baby from
Peter's arms.

"Give her to me. You can't have her. She's dead because
you weren't there. Give her to me. She's mine."

Then Peter spoke. A sudden wind blew through the
clearing, setting everything in motion, and his words travelled around on the rustle of leaves, the tapping of branches
against one another, the lap of water on the rocky shore.
They murmured through the gaps, around and around,
encircling Maggie like a whirlwind. "It didn't just happen to
you, it didn't just happen to you."

Peter faded, his features blurring, transparent. She could
see through him, the shape of the huckleberry bush behind
him, the crumbling bark of the log beneath him. Her fingers grasped at air and she cried, "Don't go, Peter." She
whispered into the empty clearing. "Please don't leave me."

Maggie fell, the moss wet on the knees of her jeans. *It
didn't just happen to you.* Peter had spoken those words to
her once before. Weeks, a month, after Angel's death, she
had woken one morning, unable to drag herself from the

bed and face the day. She had dropped into a deep black hole during the night and couldn't get out. Everything was hard; the thought of dressing exhausted her. She pulled the quilt over her head and refused to get up. Liam came repeatedly into the bedroom, tugging on the covers, calling her, "Mama, get up." When she didn't respond, he returned to the kitchen to his father. Each time, Liam's voice grew more insistent, more desperate, his tugs more forceful. Maggie couldn't bring herself to respond. Finally, Liam collapsed beside the bed. Peter picked the sobbing boy from the floor and tore the quilt from her face. "Maggie, look at us. Look at Liam and me. It didn't just happen to you. See us."

She hadn't looked at them. She hadn't seen the pain on their faces. She turned her back to them and said, "Peter, please leave me be."

They had gone away. She heard them talking in the kitchen. The outside door open, then close. Their footsteps on the deck. Then peace. She slept. By late afternoon, the black cloak of depression was gone.

She hadn't thought about that day and Peter's words until now. *It didn't just happen to you.* She thought he meant Liam had lost his sister. She had tried, after that day, to ensure Liam felt loved and cared for. But she had misunderstood. A father had also lost a daughter. Peter had lost Angel too.

The air swirled in front of her. Was Peter coming back? To receive her apology? Was she ready for that?

But it wasn't Peter. Liam and Joy materialized before her. Liam, a sad clown, his wide red mouth downturned, his eyes two soulful diamonds. A bold red-rimmed tear below his left eye. He was seated on the log, Joy standing back several paces from his left shoulder. Her face was twisted in a mixture of pain and anger. Maggie recognized it from the last time she had seen Joy. Joy had left home, angry, hurt, and she hadn't come back.

It didn't just happen to you.

Maggie held her stomach as she bent over in pain. She hadn't held her daughter in two years.

But Liam, that had been okay. He came to see her often. He and Rose. They cooked her dinner. Invited her to their apartment many times. Dozens of times.

She never went. She didn't even know what street their apartment was on.

Maggie covered her face with shaking hands. At Peter's funeral her children walked with her, one on either side, their arms under her elbows, bearing her weight, keeping her from sliding to the floor as they walked down the aisle. The organ music drew them along toward the mass of flowers and the ashes on the altar. She hadn't thought how brave they were. She hadn't thought about them for a minute. She accepted their arms and their elbows, their measured footsteps guiding hers. And after, they brought trays of food to her darkened room. For a month they hovered at her doorway, watching over her. At the end of each day they took away the untouched tray without a word. She didn't wipe a single tear from their eyes . . . she hadn't noticed they had tears. She had done the unimaginable; she had abandoned her children to their grief.

Haliaeetus leucocephalus
BALD EAGLE

An ancient snag dominates the southwest corner of the island. It's hard to miss from here on the water. Higher than all the other trees, it must be forty metres tall. Its trunk is riddled with holes from insects and woodpeckers. You can hear the woodpeckers early in the morning. The pileated are the noisiest, beating their long bills into the pithy wood, hunting for bugs, their red crests bright against the bark. The bigger holes make great nests. I think snags are the most important trees in the forest. Wildlife condominiums.

There's an eagle up there now, on the bare, dead, top branches. It's his favourite spot to sit. I'm sure he can see everything from there, three hundred and sixty degrees. Right now, he's watching us. I know Peter is watching too, from his drawing table by the library window. Joy and Liam and I floating by.

The children are jigging for cod from the rowboat. I am in charge of the oars, with orders to keep the boat away from the rocks, out of the kelp bed, before it gets too deep, not too fast, not too slow, don't rock the boat. I am behaving and the two children are diligent in their task, fishing rods held motionless over the water. Every few seconds they jerk their rod tips up, the line pulling taut, then slack, then tight again as the lure settles to the bottom.

152   I can't take my eyes off them. Liam is ten and Joy five. In spite of the years between them, they truly enjoy one another's company. Joy adores her brother. I can see it in her eyes. Even fishing she holds her arm against his leg or her foot touching his. Her big brother. Ever since she could crawl she followed him everywhere. He never complains.

Joy jumps to her feet and squeals, "I've got one."

Liam throws down his rod into the bottom of the boat and grabs the net. Joy, her tongue gripped between her teeth, winds furiously at the reel. I try to keep the boat steady. Slowly it appears to us; the flared spines and spotted scales of a rockfish, its pale yellow underbelly rolling to the surface, air bladder bulging with the unnatural rise from the depths.

Liam expertly slides the net under the fish and pulls it into the boat, smiling at his sister. "Good job, Joy."

She beams at this praise. The rockfish thrashes its head and tail vainly at the hard aluminum surface of the boat in a frantic attempt to fling itself back into the water. Its gills flap open and closed against the side of its head. Liam pulls a fishing knife from his belt and, twisting his wrist like Peter taught him, shoves the blade down between the eyes of the struggling fish. It flops from side to side against the knife, then stops thrashing. In one long motion, Liam runs the blade from gills to anus. The worms of intestine and stomach spill into a bucket, which he dumps overboard. With a gloved hand to avoid the sharp, infectious spines, he draws the knife along the back and the opaque flesh peels away in perfect fillets.

He tosses one slippery fillet to Joy and says, "You can go first, okay."

Joy scrambles to the bow of the boat and stands, her stocky legs straddling the bench seat for balance, and holds the chunk of fish in the air.

Liam lets out a sharp, prolonged whistle and whispers, "Now, Joy."

She throws the fish overhand, like a baseball, away from the boat. It lands with a smack in the water, floating lifeless before it begins to sink. We all turn toward the island and the tallest snag. But the eagle is already on his way, wings open, a good two-metre span, swooping, legs suspended, gliding from the top of the tree down to the water. He grabs the sinking morsel of fish flesh from the sea and, with one beat of his wings, pivots and climbs through the air back to his perch.

We clap and cheer. Joy bounces up and down with excitement and I have to caution her not to dump us over. We watch the eagle tear the fillet to pieces, pinning it against the branch with its talons, jabbing sharply with its curved beak at each bite. Its white head flashes in the sun.

"Your turn now, Liam," I say and he takes his place.

Like Joy, he straddles the seat and raises his hand. His whistle is strong and steady. I watch the eagle turn its head and rise from the branch, wings unfolding. It soars once again toward us. Its speed is deceptive, masked by the graceful power of a skillful hunter. Liam is still holding the fillet in his hand.

"Throw it, Liam," I call. "He's almost here."

Liam keeps his arm raised, his eyes fixed on the great raptor.

"Liam! Throw the fish!" I yell.

I can't believe what he is doing. I lunge forward to grab

him, but it is too late. The eagle is over us. Its talons wrap around the fish and Liam's hand. Joy screams. I hear the rush of wind through wing feathers as the bird launches into the air. I duck, pulling Joy down beside me, the shadow of the eagle falling across us. The boat rocks wildly.

When I recover, Liam is standing, laughing in the bow of the boat, punching his fist in the air. His face is flushed. He is grinning.

"I did it! Wasn't that incredible?" he crows.

Joy stares at him, astonished. Shaking, I reach over and pull him to me.

"You scared me to death, you crazy kid."

I grab his hand and turn it over. An angry red welt runs across his knuckles but there is no blood.

"Don't worry, Mom, it doesn't hurt," he says, his voice husky with pride, and pulls his hand back.

I put my arm around his shoulders, not knowing whether to laugh or cry. Joy squeezes in between us and joins in the hug.

"Do it again, Liam," she says.

"No way," I say. "One of those was enough for me."

"Please."

I shake my head. "Let's get home. You can tell Dad. You guys row."

Joy and Liam, their excited voices echoing across the water, row us around the island to the dock. I think about the day last spring when I watched the eagle hunt a mother mallard and her ducklings. There were eight of them, fluffy little yellow and brown things, swimming across the north end of the cove. The eagle dove at them repeatedly. The flock should have been an easy target. He tried at least a dozen times. At each attempt, the mother duck dove at the last minute and her ducklings followed, one after another, like beads on a string. The eagle went hungry that after-noon, not because he wasn't a good hunter, but because of the invisible thread between the mother and her babies.

I watch my own ducklings, straining at the wooden oars, laughing as our little boat twirls in a circle because Joy has stopped rowing to scratch her nose. I know I will never lose that thread, that unspoken conversation with my children. I simply know. I will always be there for them, to pull them to safety, like that mother mallard.

"Hey, Liam." I need to tell him. "That was incredible."

He stops rowing to raise his arm once more in a victory salute. As the boat spins, we see the eagle on its perch, tear-ing at the fish with its powerful talons, bits of flesh falling from the crown branch to the ground at the bottom of the snag.

155

TWELVE

Maggie whispered to the young before her, "Can you forgive me?"

Liam, the sad clown, the tearful joker, looked to his left and Rose materialized out of the night. Kind, gentle Rose, her mass of dark hair pulled back sensibly from her round, friendly face. She held a baby. Angel? No, a chubby, curly-haired girl. So like Liam as an infant. Rose placed the child in Liam's lap. The baby squealed, delighted. Liam held her up to Maggie, inviting his mother to hold her grandchild in her arms.

Maggie hesitated and when she reached out to receive the child, her hands met only air.

The chatter of a kingfisher and the damp of the morning dew drew Maggie from sleep. She shivered from the cold and the memory of the night. Could it have been a dream? She raised her head, her neck stiff, and looked for evidence of her night's encounter. For signs of her family. A footprint? A fallen strand of hair? Instead, she saw flowers. A clump of Indian pipe at the base of the rotting log, in the spot where Peter's feet had rested. And beyond, in the wild grasses where Joy had stood, a single pink fairyslipper orchid.

The two flowers bowed their graceful heads to one another, mirror images. One phantom white, inhabiting the darkest hollows of the deep forest, scavenging sustenance from decomposing litter and rotting carcasses of trees. *Monotropa uniflora*, Indian pipe, corpse plant. The other, infused with colour and vigour, thriving at the edge of the sea, where light holds back the shadows. *Calypso bulbosa*, fairyslipper, goddess of love.

Maggie reached up to brush the hair from her eyes. The pulpy body of a slug fell from her brow. She recoiled at its texture and the thought of it in her hair. She ran one hand down a cheek, expecting an absence of sensation, but the flesh was warm and supple. The images of her family swirled in confusion with the white and pink of the flowers that, merely by their presence, seemed to demand a decision.

Even now, the grey mist of grief occupied her. Would these hands stain the perfect skin of a newborn with sorrow and discontent? She shivered.

Maggie knelt and dug her fingers deep into the moss. Indian pipe, fairyslipper. What to choose? She was ashamed to read guilt within her own heart.

THIRTEEN

Maggie stood surrounded by the rubble of the cupboard. Fragments of oak wood were strewn in violent heaps across the living room floor, shards of fine mahogany inlay visible in the wreckage. The axe rested in the middle of the debris. She turned her hands, palm to back, back to palm, in wonderment at the power hidden under the wrinkles and the pale skin . . . the frightening possibilities. She had proven herself capable of many frightening things these past years. Murder, abandonment, near suicide. What is a cupboard compared to the lives she had shattered?

She picked up the axe and ran her finger along the blade. Her touch released a faint tone, like the rim of a crystal glass when stroked. As if it were alive. Maggie dropped it to the floor and covered her ears with her hands. The tone persisted and grew louder.

Alan Page walked onto the deck outside the kitchen. He was whistling, the casual, relaxed sound of a happy man on his way to complete an enjoyable job. Pausing at the top of the garden steps, he glanced through the window. When he saw Maggie, he stopped whistling. Then he was in the room with her.

"What the hell has happened here?"

Maggie surrounded by chaos, an axe at her feet, could not meet his eyes.

"What's going on? Are you all right?"

Maggie turned in a slow circle, surveying the room, seeing the disaster as if for the first time, as if through Alan's eyes. She ran her hands across her head. Bits of twig and moss were tangled in knots of hair. Her arms were scratched and dry with blood. Was her face as bad? Did slugs and ants continue to travel her body?

Alan gripped her shoulder and asked again, "Maggie, what is it, who did this?"

She leaned into him and he steadied her as she slid to the floor. Words spilled from her mouth, the dam of years broken, words tumbling across and around one another in waves. "I went to the forest. To die. I couldn't do it. I'm too weak."

"You spent the night in the forest?" he said.

"Not like Peter. I'm not strong like him." Maggie was crying now.

"Peter? Is there someone else here? Is he the one who made this mess?"

"No, I did it. With the axe. Peter was in the forest. He wouldn't let me die."

"Maggie!" With both hands, Alan turned her face to meet his eyes. "Who the hell is Peter?"

"My husband," she whispered.

"Your husband? But he's—" Alan paled.

Maggie sobbed. "I killed him. My children . . . I abandoned them. I was only thinking of myself. I don't deserve to live. But I couldn't do it. I couldn't do it."

He crouched beside her, his arms around her heaving shoulders. For a long time he rocked her, stroking her hair with his calloused palm, and listened to her confused rambling fade into an exhausted hush.

When she stopped crying, he lifted her to her feet and carried her to the kitchen. He propped her in a chair at the table, squeezed her shoulders and walked away. She could hear the sound of water splashing into stainless steel. Then his footsteps down the hall to the bathroom. Beside her, the window framed an idyllic spring day.

161

Alan returned with a bowl of warm water, a hairbrush and a towel. He washed her cheeks, working gently around the long scratches. He washed the smear of dirt from her forehead, the crust of blood from her arms, the grime from between her fingers. He pulled the hairbrush through her mass of hair, long, graceful sweeps from the crown of her head, teasing apart each mat. A mound of moss and twigs grew on the table. Maggie relaxed into the massage of bristles on her scalp. His hands against her skin were comforting. Neither of them spoke. He tied her hair from her face with a length of string and then walked back to the kitchen counter.

Maggie heard the grinding rasp of a can opener, the clank of pots, the hiss of the propane stovetop. The smell of food. He brought a bowl of thick black bean soup, a plate of buttered bread and a steaming cup of tea to the table and pulled up a chair beside her. He fed her spoonful by spoonful, blowing on each mouthful as she used to feed her toddlers. When the bowl was empty, he placed the slice of bread into her hand and once again was gone.

The heat from the soup felt good. The feeling returned to her fingers and feet. She bit into the heavy bread, then laid it on the table beside the cup of tea. She listened for

Alan. The silence unnerved her. He wouldn't, couldn't leave her here now. But there he was, walking up the bedroom stairs with an armful of folded clothes from her backpack: a fresh white t-shirt, jeans, underwear, a sweater. Bending down on one knee, he removed her shoes, then her socks. He lifted her to standing and slid off her soiled, torn jeans, and one by one undid the buttons of her shirt. He placed her clean clothes on the table and turned away.

162

Maggie watched him as she dressed. Even with his back turned, he released an aura of calm into the room. This stranger, this good man. For the first time since Peter's death, she longed for the gaze of a man on her body. If only as proof she was alive and a woman.

The ache in Maggie's joints was enough to prove to herself that she was alive. Her back, her shoulders, her fingers screamed as she negotiated through pant legs, zippers, sleeves and buttons. She fumbled with the last of the buttons on her sweater and sat down with relief.

"I'm done," she said.

He smiled and knelt in front of her, pulling woollen socks over her feet. After tying her shoes, he reached out his hand and said, "I want to show you something."

She didn't ask where they were going, and he didn't tell her. He led her from the house and down the trail to the dock. It didn't occur to Maggie to do anything but trust. The way her children used to trust her—with innocence. He arranged a blanket in the bottom of the canoe and balanced two lifejackets against the back of the bow seat, then helped her to settle against them, facing him in the stern. He pushed the canoe from the dock and paddled northwest. She could tell he was a skilled canoeist by the way he feathered the paddle, altering their course with an almost unnoticeable pause at the end of every stroke. He appeared at home out here on the water. As they glided along the shoreline, she noticed his eyes were dusty green like the lichens that dangled from the overhanging trees. Exhausted, Maggie relaxed into the rhythm of the dipping paddle and the sound of water flowing past the boat hull. Oddly content, she dropped her life, for this moment, into Alan's hands.

163

Alan navigated the canoe out of the cove and into the channel. The day was fair and calm, the sea silver in the sun like liquid blue mercury. A glassy wave curled away from the bow of the boat in two thick ribbons of shimmering water. Maggie shielded her eyes from the sun, grateful for the warmth on her face, the effort of the night pooling in her limbs.

She knew this stretch of coastline well. It was a place she had often come, where great heaps of rocks the size of cars had fallen from the high cliffs and lay jumbled half in and half out of the sea. At low tide, purple and orange seastars hung among the limp strands of brown and green seaweed draping the rocks. Harbour seals hauled out on the shelves and ledges formed by the giant boulders.

"Look," Alan called quietly.

Maggie sat up and followed the line of his pointing finger. Five harbour seals lolled on the sandstone ledge. The tiny wavelets that always lived at the edge of sea and land lapped below their sleek, rotund bodies. Cautious brown eyes peered over long, bristly whiskers at Alan and Maggie. As if annoyed at the intrusion, the animals squirmed and humped themselves awkwardly into the sea.

Alan gestured to the other side of the canoe. Two seals, their spotted grey and white heads, shiny with water, observed the boat from the edge of a bull kelp forest, their eyes at water level, unblinking, sharply exhaling through flaring nostrils. Alan slid his paddle into the water and the canoe drifted toward the seals. The larger of the two rose up and, with an explosion of white spray, was gone. The smaller head remained. A pup. It swam in circles, gasping for breath, frantic for its mother, drawing closer and closer to the canoe with every turn. Maggie and Alan sat motionless, barely daring to breathe. Maggie could see the glint of light and fear in its eyes, each fine, wet hair of its white and smoke coat, the thick wrinkles of insulating fat under the skin. It turned once again and at the apex of its turn collided with the hull of the canoe. Maggie flinched at the impact of skull against solid fibreglass. The vibration travelled along the boat and through her body. The pup sank below the surface and turned on its back to reveal the white ribbon of an umbilical cord trailing behind.

The umbilical cord. It pulled her back to the memory of her own children's birth. The pulsing of the cord, her babies slippery with vernix between her legs, not yet ready to loose themselves from her. The thick, snaking vein that throbbed with her blood, the thread that held mother and child together. The moment of severance, the original act of separation.

The mother seal watched from a distance.

"Back up," Maggie said.

The boat glided away from the struggling infant. The mother dove, surfacing to support her baby on her back, and the pair disappeared into a crevice in the rocks.

The cave was unexpected. Maggie had paddled this shore dozens of times, at all heights of tides, and she had never found this cave. Alan obviously knew it well. He paddled straight toward the cliff. At the instant before impact, a narrow opening emerged and the canoe slipped from sunlight to shadow.

It was more like a room than a true cave. An enormous flat rock spanned two jumbled columns of boulders to form a roof, its underside worn into a curved bowl by waves and salt water on sandstone. Water dripped onto the top of Maggie's head and she looked up. As her eyes adjusted to the dim light, she saw, not hard, brown sandstone, but textures, colours and movement. Seastars, anemones, mussels, barnacles, spider crabs, nudibranchs—the life of the deeper intertidal zone, accessible only at the lowest of tides. She heard the rustle of barnacles snapping their trap doors shut to hold in moisture, and the scuttle of shore and hermit crabs through the mass of arms and legs that crowded the rock face at least a hand-span thick.

"It's amazing," she said.

Alan grabbed a kelp crab from an iridescent brown frond of seaweed hanging above his head and smiled. "It's what everything is all about," he said.

Holding the crab by the rear to avoid the pinch of the heavy claws, he stroked the olive green carapace with his finger.

"When my daughter Lisa died, I felt like you do now. I don't know how I made the decision to come to the island. The entire ferry trip, I stood out on the deck, leaning over the railing, staring at the water and thinking how easy it would be to swing my leg over and let go."

"What stopped you?" Maggie asked.

He laughed. "I guess it would have been a damn cold and slow way to die . . . " He paused.

Maggie knew what he wasn't saying and flushed. *Like lying in the woods?*

"I don't know why I didn't. Lisa wouldn't have wanted me to, I guess. I kept thinking about the look in her eyes before she died. She trusted me to make everything better. Like I could fix anything."

"What about your wife?"

He was quiet for a moment; the crab in his hands waved its long pincers through the air. "We didn't make it much more than a few months together. I think about that a lot. I thought we were close. But we weren't there for each other. She became frantic about life and threw herself into doing things. She couldn't bear to be in the house anymore. I wanted to lie low and ruminate. I guess we grieved in different ways. One day she was gone."

"And then you came over here?"

He nodded. "A couple of weeks after she left. When I got off the ferry I rented a kayak and started paddling like a madman around the islands. I had some crazy idea I'd find a deserted island, like yours, and become a hermit. Instead I found this cave. I was captivated by this place and for a few minutes, I forgot all about my daughter and my pain, and well, as they say, the rest is history."

Maggie stretched her hand up and touched the rough surface of a purple seastar. It clung upside down with another half dozen of its kind. It was alive, gripping on to life day by day, doing what seastars do, its millions of little tube feet propelling it along the rock face. Hunting, feeding, moving, reproducing. Did seastars sleep? Did one seastar need another the way humans needed one another? Liam had told her seastars could regenerate an arm, or grow an entire body from one limb. She wished she knew their secret. It was going to be a long, difficult job to grow back the limbs she had lost when Peter died.

Alan draped a strand of feather boa kelp around his neck, and dropped the crab on his head, its pincers raised and open in self-defense. For the first time in a long time, Maggie laughed aloud.

"Do you know Paula Fletcher?" she said, surprised at her own question.

"Yes, I do. Her husband and I are in the fire department," he said. He lifted the crab from his hair and returned it to the slick surface of the kelp frond. "Is she a friend of yours?"

"Yes ... well, we used to be friends. How is she?"

"As far as I know, she's fine. She and her husband raise chickens."

"Yes, I know ... knew that? I ... think I'd like to call her. Would you mind if I came and used your phone? Tomorrow morning. Would that be all right?"

"Of course," Alan said. He back-paddled the canoe out of the cave and into brilliant sunshine. "Any time."

A warmth spread through Maggie at the thought of Paula's arms around her. She reclined onto the lifejackets and closed her eyes to the sun. "Yes, I'd like to call her. Tomorrow."

They explored far down the Galiano coastline and it was dark when Alan left her on the island dock. He insisted on walking her up to the house, but she refused.

"You haven't got a flashlight," he said.

"I don't need one. This path is as familiar to me as my own hand," she said.

"Tomorrow then," he said. He lowered his kayak into the

water, disturbing the tiny bioluminescent plankton that emitted flashes of light into the space between dock and boat. His rudder left a sparkling trail that followed him across the moonless cove. She watched until the light was gone, then turned to feel her way up the path.

BIOLUMINESCENCE

I wonder if my life is simply the imaginings of a great being, far beyond my limits of comprehension. This being—a woman perhaps—has looked kindly on me and granted me the gift of a perfect moment.

I lie suspended in the universe; above me stars, below me stars. At the end of my outstretched arms are my children: Liam to my right, Joy to my left. Peter floats at my feet. We are touching, finger to finger, toe to toe. The sea is cold, but we are oblivious to it, for we are preoccupied with the light. Each time we move—one of us moves—there is an explosion from the inky darkness below us. Microscopic bodies, disturbed, tumble away from us, flashing through the midnight water of the cove, which appears empty but is chock full of life. Plankton, luminescent plankton.

We laugh. At the wonder of it all, at each other, lying here in the glassy sea, the night sky splendid above us. A minute ago we were in the canoe, paddling home from dinner with neighbours, exclaiming at the green glowing wave sweeping from the bow as the boat sliced through the dark canvas of the cove. Our paddles, like magic wands, sketched sparkling trails alongside.

Peter let out a wild whoop and he was in the water, his body a shimmering outline. Joy and Liam yelled and leaped overboard after him. I scolded them for getting their clothes soaked. Then their hands were on the gunwale of the canoe, pulling it down, the three of them howling like pirates. The canoe capsized. Seawater flooded in, swirling around my skirt. Then I was swimming too.

We swam together, the four of us, the glowing plankton falling in shining droplets from our arms, a wave of tumbling radiance before us. The children splashed one another, each glimmering sheet rolling up into the air and over them. They shrieked with the sting of cold and the excitement of it all.

Without speaking, we formed a pattern with our bodies—floating, touching, awed. We aren't separate people; we are part of one glorious shining universe.

Where's Peter? The spot at my feet where he was floating is glowing. It fades and smoothes into endless black. I tread water and turn, scanning for him. A bright sphere, like a burning comet, cascades towards me. His arms are around me, lifting me upward, against him, his mouth on mine. Before he pulls me under, we hear the giggling of the children.

FOURTEEN

*Right on Seaview Drive, right after you cross the creek, left down
the long driveway at the big arbutus, park at the end of the road,
take the path directly ahead through the woods, I'll be waiting
with coffee, if you miss the house you'll be in the drink.*

Maggie walked from the beach to the car. She rehearsed
the directions Alan had given her on the dock the previous
night. Finding directions on the island was not a linear
process like in the city with its streets laid out in neat blocks
and numbered houses, plotted carefully on a map. Here you
felt your way through the dark. Intuition was essential. One
had to pay attention to the nuances of the road, landmarks
along the way. Each stump, each curve, the pattern of the sun
on the asphalt as it filtered down through the branches, could
be a signpost, convey an important meaning, a subtle change
in the journey. If missed, you could find yourself driving
down a dead end or wandering lost through the forest.

She found the house easily. Alan's directions were trustworthy; he was trustworthy. Solid. Reliable. She knew little

about him, but that quivering, frightened place within her had settled yesterday when she was with him in the canoe. She found herself looking forward to their meeting this morning. It was unnerving, this pull toward another man. Peter was gone. Yet she felt like a cheating wife, betraying her husband, betraying his memory, to have this thought of another man's hands upon her. What was she frightened of? Would she forget? Would the strands of Peter that inhabited her body, her mind, be replaced by those of another man? Peter had been her orientation for so many years.

172

She stopped at the edge of the woods. The dark coolness of the forest opened into a bright expanse of meadow, the path leading through shin-high grass to a haphazard drift-wood fence. The gate was open, inviting. She could turn back, into the past, the muted, dim silence of the forest. Or take one step forward and another. She blushed. She was being foolish; she had simply come to make a phone call.

Alan greeted her at the door and thrust a steaming cup of coffee into her outstretched hand. He stepped back to let her in. He looked relaxed, the tails of a brushed cotton shirt hanging down over baggy, faded sweatpants.

"Welcome to my humble abode," he said, bowing low.

Maggie stepped through the doorway and walked over to the picture window occupying the entire southwest wall.

"You forgot one important item in your directions," she said as she peered down at the sea slapping the rocks directly below the house. "Before the 'in the drink' part. You left out the terrifying fall."

"Yes, well. I didn't want to scare you away," he said. "Definitely not."

"Compared to this," she said, "the slope on the island is practically horizontal. I'm not sure if you're courageous or naïve. It must be wild here in a storm."

"It's magnificent. As for whether I'm courageous or naïve, I'll leave that judgement up to you," he said.

Maggie turned from the window to look around the room. "Your house, it's unusual. Did you build it?" she asked.

"Yep, every board came out of the salt chuck. I used a chainsaw mill to cut it up. Don't tell the building inspector, though. He wouldn't approve of the setback from the cliff." Alan took her hand and pulled her into the centre of the floor. "Come on. I'll give you the grand tour."

173

Maggie laughed. The house was a single room, cozy and intimate, everything visible in a turn. A counter and sink ran along the back wall. The simple cabinets were crafted with skill; the doors shone with the warm hue of hand-finished wood. A bentwood rocking chair, the seat and back covered with quilted cushions, sat beside an airtight stove. Firelight flickered through the soot-veiled glass doors; a dented aluminum coffee pot bubbled on the cast-iron cooktop. The room smelled like coffee and cedar. She could see an outhouse through the back window, half buried in salal, no door.

A number of unfinished sandstone carvings and a few tools sat on a hand-hewn table under the picture window.

"You didn't tell me you were a sculptor," Maggie said.

"Correction. Trying to be a sculptor," Alan said. "I play around with it. That's all."

Maggie picked up one of the sandstone pieces, a figurine of a female. It made her think of Joy, or herself as a young girl. It had a primitive quality, the lines simple, almost archetypal. "Well, keep on playing. I love it."

"You can have it," he said.

"Really?"

He reached out and ran his fingers across her cheek. "I'd like you to have it. It would be an honour."

Maggie took a step back, away from his touch. "I . . . can't—"

He dropped his hand to his side. His eyes held no embarrassment, his gaze steady and calm. Maggie turned nervously and walked to the far end of the house. A queen-size bed built of curved slabs of driftwood and covered with a counterpane quilt of mermaids and fish dominated the space. Wooden tracks ran across the floor from the foot of the bed to the wall where a large window overlooked the sea. The legs were mounted on wheels. Maggie tilted her head quizzically at Alan.

"Go stand at the window and watch this," he said.

He pushed on the heavy frame and the bed rolled along the tracks until it hit the wall below the window. A section of wall swung up and out and the bed slid through.

"Where did it go?" Maggie ran over to the window. The bed rested outside on a small, cantilevered deck.

"I prefer to sleep outside." Allan grinned. "Like it? You get to the deck out the side door. And don't worry. It's architecturally sound."

Maggie shook her head. "You're full of surprises. I hope one of those surprises isn't that you don't actually have a phone."

"Have no fear, madam." He pointed toward the kitchen. "It's my one modern convenience. On the wall beside the door."

Maggie had forgotten Paula's number. She stood in front of the phone, rattled by the realization. Paula's number should have been carved into her brain from years of constant use. She searched the kitchen for a phone book and found the Galiano Island Directory on the counter under

Alan's sweater and a *Fine Homebuilding* magazine. She fumbled through the pages. Fletcher, Paula and Lester. Her finger trembled as she dialled the number. Her earlier confidence was replaced by apprehension. What if Paula didn't want to see her? Why would she? The phone rang once and Maggie hung up. She leaned her forehead against the wall. She'd chased her away. She'd chased them all away.

She stared blankly at the phone for several minutes, then dialled Liam's number.

"Mom?" He sounded anxious. "Is everything okay?"

"Yes," she said. "I'm fine. The house is ready. I should be back to Vancouver day after tomorrow."

"Oh good." She heard the relief in his voice. "I was starting to wonder. I didn't know if it was the right thing. For me to pressure you like that, I mean."

"No, it was right, Liam." She couldn't tell him about the broken cabinet, about her night in the forest. "I'm glad I came."

"And Dad?" he said. "Did you—"

"Not yet. I plan to do that tomorrow."

"You are all right, aren't you, Mom?"

"Yes, dear. And how is Rose?"

"Well, other than the constant nausea, she's wonderful."

"Tell her raspberry leaf tea is good for morning sickness. And the baby?"

"We saw the doctor yesterday. We had an ultrasound. We could see the fingers and toes. It was unbelievable. They asked us if we wanted to know the sex. But we didn't. We wanted it to stay a surprise. The doctor said everything was on schedule."

"I'm glad, sweetie. I never wanted to know the sex, either. It didn't matter." She paused. "Liam?"

"Yes, Mom." The anxious tone was back. "Something's wrong, I know it."

"No, it's . . . could you give me Joy's phone number, please?"

He didn't answer right away. "Yeah," he said. "Yeah, sure. She's still at Uncle Mark's. Do you remember his number?"

"Oh, yes, of course. I wasn't sure if she was still there. I do remember it."

"You're going to call her now? Today?"

"Right now."

"Mom."

"Yes, honey."

"You might have to give her time."

Time. It had already been far too long a time.

"Thanks, Liam," she said. "I'll call you when I get back."

Maggie hung up the phone and stared at a knot in the wall. She bit her lip and dialled Mark's number in East Vancouver. The phone rang twice before a man answered. She recognized Mark's steady voice immediately.

"Hello, may I speak with Joy, please," Maggie mumbled, hoping he wouldn't know it was her.

"Joy? Yes, just a min— Is this Maggie?"

"Yes, it is," she said, her hand trembled, the receiver shook against her cheek. "Hello, Mark."

"Well, well. This is a surprise. It's about time." He had always been polite, the kind of person who would go out of his way to avoid confrontation. Maggie prayed he wouldn't ask her any questions. She was relieved when he said, "Listen, it's good to hear from you. Really good. I'll get Joy for you. She's just getting ready for work."

"Thank you, Mark." She waited. She could hear household noises: a radio, a door slamming, the clatter of someone picking up the phone.

"Maggie?" It was Mark. "Joy won't . . . she can't come to the phone right—" Maggie heard angry voices in the background. Then the rasp of tense breathing on the line.

"Mark? Joy?"

"It's Joy." Her daughter's voice was flat and hard.

"This is Mom, dear." Maggie pressed her fingers against her lips to keep herself from crying.

"I know who it is."

"I know it's been a long time. I can tell you're still mad. I don't blame you."

Joy didn't answer. But there was no click, no hum of a broken connection.

"Joy. Are you there? I want to see you. We need to see each other." Maggie twisted the phone cord around her wrist.

Nothing.

"Joy, I've been wrong. I was selfish. I didn't think about you or anybody else. I'm sorry, Joy. Please, I need to—I want to see you."

"Where are you?" Joy's voice was guarded.

"I'm on Galiano."

"Galiano?"

"Yes, it's a long story. Didn't Liam tell you?"

"Tell me what? Nobody tells me anything," she snapped.

Maggie braced herself for the storm. "I'm . . . I'm scattering Dad's ashes tomorrow. I'll be home in a couple of days. Please, I need to see you."

"What if I don't need to see you?"

"Okay. I won't pressure you. This has all been my fault. Tell you what. You call me. Next week. I'll wait for you to phone."

Joy sniffled on the other end of the line. The plaintive sound of a hurt child. Maggie listened to it helplessly. She couldn't reach out across Georgia Strait and stroke her hair, kiss the pain away, comfort her. The way a mother—a good mother—would do for her child. How could she project that longing through a few wires?

"Joy, please speak to me, say something."

Nothing.

178   "Joy . . . I'm going to hang up now. Goodbye, dear." Maggie said and pulled the receiver from her ear.

"Mom!" Joy yelled, the word clear in the silence of Alan's kitchen.

Maggie pressed the phone back against her ear. "Joy?"

"You call me," Joy said and hung up.

Maggie stood, the receiver in her hand, the dial tone buzzing, the cord still curled around her wrist. *You call me.* It was as much as she could hope for, after all this time. Hope. There had been hope in Joy's hurried order, hadn't there? She placed the receiver on its cradle and looked out to mid-channel where a tugboat churned the water into froth as it hauled a log boom against the tide.

"Hope," she whispered to herself.

Alan was on the deck sweeping fir needles from the drift-wood planks. She paused before stepping onto the precari-ous platform. Alan heard her and turned.

"Don't worry. I have it on good authority that it won't go plunging down the cliff. I sleep out here most nights it doesn't rain. Even then." He pointed up to an awning rolled against the window frame.

Maggie walked to the railing. The sea sloshed in and out between the barnacle-crusted rocks at the bottom of the cliff. Stonecrop clung tenaciously to pockets and ledges in the cliffside, surviving, thriving on its succulent leaves in a few teaspoonfuls of dry soil. She understood why Alan lived here. He was a survivor who had seen death and knew it couldn't beat him. Nothing to lose, living on the edge, free of fear. She grasped the railing and leaned over until her hips met wood. The railing was solid; like Alan, she could let herself lean into its support, trusting it would hold her. She pushed herself upright. It also took luck to live at the edge of an abyss without falling. Grabbing on to life, taking what it offered. Alan swept a pile of needles and dirt under the railing. It cascaded into mid-air and down, like a water-fall of grit, vanishing as it fell, dust to air.

179

"About as far down as jumping off a ferry, don't you think?" he said.

Maggie tried not to smile at his morbid humour.

Liam would like it here: the freedom, the daring fancy of it. She wasn't so sure about Joy. Joy needed nightlife and people her own age. What did she know about Joy's needs? And Peter? He would appreciate the skill and creativity that went into this house. But he would need more space, wouldn't he? What would he say if he was standing before her now? Would he find the house romantic? Or would he tell her it was foolish? That this building didn't belong here, another blight on paradise. She didn't know anymore, what Peter would say. Would he invite her to come with him, hold his hand out to her? She squeezed her eyes shut and imagined sliding her hand into his. Is this not what she had wanted? To be with him, to be one again. She watched her hand disappear into Peter's, like a shadow overwhelmed by bright sunlight. Like their marriage. She the shadow, Peter the sun. Not a merging, but a swallowing up. If she continued, walked forward into his arms, she would vanish along with her hand. Maggie would be gone.

She snatched her hand away and held it against her face.

Even with her eyes closed, she knew the lifelines on her palm, the veins under her skin, the folds in the joints.

"Maggie?" Alan's voice tugged her from the daydream. She opened her eyes, his face framed by her fingers.

"It's not safe to walk around out here with your eyes closed," he said. He stood between her and the railing. He pulled her hand from her face and cupped it in his palm. Maggie stared at their hands, skin to skin, intact, separate, yet together, warm flesh on warm flesh.

She twined her fingers through his. "I'm glad you didn't jump from the ferry," she said. "You do plan to stay around for a while, don't you?"

He laughed. "Absolutely, unless you throw me over the railing."

She stepped forward into his arms. The water heaved and rolled beneath them. The waves gurgled as they threaded into the openings between the boulders and back out again. A kingfisher chattered in a tree somewhere nearby. Gentle heat from the spring sun was on her face. Tension undid inside her, like the bow on a child's shoelace, innocently slipping apart, opening a space previously controlled by knots and string, now uncontrollable. *Peter is gone, Maggie.* She felt the muscles in Alan's back beneath his shirt. His fingers trickled through her hair. He smelled like his house: coffee and woodsmoke.

She kissed his fingers. They were calloused, alive. She drew him to the bed and sat down, then undid the lace on one shoe. He knelt and peered into her eyes, his own full of questions.

She nodded. He bent forward, his hair brushing her knee, and continued what she had begun. He loosened the laces on her shoes and pulled them from her feet; they fell with a thud to the deck. He slipped the socks over her heels, massaging her arches and toes as they came free. He worked his way up her body, removing each piece of clothing as if it were fragile, carefully folding them in a pile on the floor beside him. The whole time he whispered to her like the wind.

Maggie took him into her arms. It was like taking in the sea, the tide rolling into her, filling her with a delicate power. She drifted, suspended in liquid, her hair flaring out from her head, each strand undulating like seaweed, gleaming copper against the blue-green cast of the water. She stole air from the sea like a fish.

They made love in the bed overhanging the cliff and then slept, the dried salt of sea spray and tears on their faces.

FIFTEEN

Maggie turned from Seaview Drive onto the main road. She felt a surge of heat run down her spine. She had forgotten this wonderful feeling of satiation that cloaked a body after making love; every cell charged with life, yet content to drift. She realized how much she had missed human contact, how much she had isolated herself from the possibility of a connection, a touch, a glance that would bring the world of another human into her own. In her grief had been the notion she was occupied, full with the loss of Peter, no room for anyone else. Alan had found a tiny space in her preoccupation. One finger running through her hair.

Maggie was startled to realize she was no longer on the main road. Her reverie had sent her down a narrow gravel track. Broom and oceanspray branches scraped along the side of the car. Its frame rattled and shook as it jostled through potholes filled with rainwater and bumped over rocks the size of a man's fist. The road had not been graded in a long time.

She watched for a wide spot in which to turn around; there was nothing but the single track winding through the woods. She carried on. The road felt familiar but it wasn't until the car rounded the final turn that she realized where she was. Fletcher's Range Eggs. Paula's house. She must have, in her distraction, turned down Paula's road, the remnant of an old habit. Was this her subconscious toying with her, navigating the car while her thoughts were back with Alan? Reminding her of unresolved business?

The yard was empty. The house hadn't changed. It was half finished like many owner-built island homes, a partial deck off the side with no railings, a stretch of cedar siding missing, torn black tarpaper dangling from the wall. The big maple sheltered the kitchen porch where Paula washed and packed eggs. Laundry hung on the line in the yard: Lester's overalls, a couple of sheets, a few t-shirts. She could hear the lazy croon of the chickens in the large coop off to the left of the driveway.

Now that she was here, Maggie felt the same misgivings. What if Paula didn't want to see her? She couldn't bring herself to walk across the yard to the porch, to call out a greeting. It had been too long. She had been cruel. Paula would never forgive her. Not after so many unanswered phone calls, the unacknowledged letters, the barricade she had erected around herself. Paula would be right to keep her at bay, like Joy. Maggie turned and put one leg back inside the car. She might not even be home.

A screen door creaked open and slammed shut. Maggie paused halfway into the car. A woman ran down the porch steps. It was Paula. She hurried across the straggly lawn, half walking, half running, her fair hair long and loose around her proud shoulders, her gaze never straying from Maggie. She drew closer and Maggie was caught by the light in her eyes. Paula stopped a few steps away. She was breathing hard, her chest rising and falling under the bleached denim of her shirt.

"I knew you would come," Paula said.

She took the last few steps and drew Maggie into her arms. Paula's embrace was strong and firm, secure. A low murmur hummed from her chest and vibrated through Maggie's body. For the second time in one day Maggie felt the grounded warmth of unconditional acceptance. She knew she had been wrong to ever doubt this woman, to reject her offerings of herself. This time she returned the embrace and the two women stood together for several minutes before they stepped back, holding one another at arm's length, and began laughing and crying and talking all at once.

"I knew it. I never gave up."

"I couldn't see you. I—"

"You're here now, that's all that matters."

"I burned your letters."

"It's okay. You needed time, that's all. Let me look at you." Paula gathered Maggie's hands in hers. "We're both getting older, aren't we?"

Strands of silver mingled with Paula's flaxen hair. She looked like a Nordic queen. Her body had broadened and shifted, like a house settling on its foundation. She was no longer the forest nymph dancing with Maggie and their toddlers under the cedar boughs, wildflowers in her hair. She had descended to earth, grounded.

"You look wonderful, Paula. What must you think of me?" Maggie said, covering her face with her hands.

Paula shook her head. "You're tired, that's all. Soul-tired. It shows on your face. But you're still you, Maggie. Nothing some loving won't fix." Paula hugged her again. "Come on, I'll make you a cup of my magic tea."

They drank tea under the maple tree and talked, a fili-
gree of sunlight through leaves dancing across them. It was
like old times. The chickens were the same, chirring and
clucking around them. The only thing missing was the children playing at their feet. It was comfortable, like the years
of grief and estrangement had never happened. Two
friends, gabbing about life. This friendship was more forgiving than any marriage, than a relationship between
mother and child. It contained less risk, more room. This
dear woman across from her, who never let her down. She
regretted the years they had lost. Paula was right. It didn't
matter. They were here now together.

"Where are the kids?" Maggie said.

"Kids no more. Sarah's in Montreal, at McGill, studying
journalism. Caleb is working at a restaurant in Victoria. I
hardly ever see them. Liam and Joy?"

"Liam's a clown. Whoever would have guessed? He has a
nice girlfriend," Maggie said. She paused. "I'm going to be
a grandmother."

Paula clapped her hands together. "You beat me. When?"

"Fall, I guess."

"You must be thrilled."

Maggie thought for a moment and nodded. "Yes. Yes, I
am."

"And Joy?"

"Joy and I haven't seen one another for a few years."
Maggie choked on the words. "Oh, Paula, I don't think she
wants to see me. I was awful to her, awful."

Paula picked up Maggie's hand and pulled it into her lap.
"She'll come back. Give her time." She hesitated, her eyes
following the jerky motion of a chicken pecking at the
ground at her feet. " Maggie, are you going to move back?"

Maggie was shaken by the question. "You mean here? To

Galiano? I hadn't thought about it? I . . . I don't know."

"I keep hoping you will," Paula said. "I miss you."

"The island and the house are sold."

"I know. I heard. I imagine that's why you're here."

"Yes." Maggie paused. "And to scatter Peter's ashes."

"Good," Paula said, stroking Maggie's fingers. "Peter needs to come home too. Have you already done it?"

"Tomorrow."

"Would you like me to come with you?"

Maggie considered the question, the offer from a friend. But it was clear what she had to do. "No, I need to do this alone. To say goodbye. Just Peter and me."

SIXTEEN

Maggie tucked a jaunty yellow blossom of Scotch broom
into the top weave of the basket on the desk and stepped
back. It wasn't exactly a masterpiece but it was finished.
The sea lettuce had cracked again, even when doubled up
and dried overnight in the mudroom. But with its array of
adornments—tassels of mussel and cockle shells, a honeysuckle vine and a frond of maidenhair fern twisted through
the bull kelp, and a rock crab claw for a wobbly handle, it
had a whimsical, happy look. The final touch—gay clusters
of blue-eyed Mary poking from the cracks. Candlelight
flickered green-gold through the layers of sea lettuce. It
was ready.

She slid the kelp and cedar basket with Peter's ashes from
the back of the desk and placed it beside her new creation.
She lifted out the candle and the gold-foil box and set them
aside, then lined both baskets with arbutus bark and moss.
She divided the ash from the box equally between them.
One for Peter. One for her.

Maggie looked up. Out the back window of the bedroom, patches of blue sky filled in the spaces between the thick canopy of branches. She could make out the eagle's nest, a two-metre-diameter oval of sticks that grew bigger each season. This time of year, there should be a chick or two in the nest. They would be close to adult size. She could hear the sharp, high trill of the adults talking to one another.

Eagles mate for life. One day in late winter, when she and the children were beachcombing after a storm, she had watched them. Two mature eagles, their white heads stark against the thin blue of the sky, their wings outstretched, riding the warm thermal currents of the rare sun of that winter day. Soaring, circling around one another, like a ballet on air. Without warning, they came together, violently, talons on talons, twirling, locked together, spiralling, falling, hurtling towards the earth. The instant before impact with the flat, glassy surface of the sea, they separated and climbed to soar, independent once again. That is what life together was, wasn't it? Taking the risk of being close to another, the risk of being separate. Together and alone.

Outside, the compact form of a young eagle chick watched from the nest, hovering on the edge, ready to soar out over the trees on its fledgling flight. She was sure the adults would be close by, vigilant. As she had failed to be for her children's first flight from home. Maggie ached to think of Joy receiving her high school diploma, knowing her mother was at home weaving baskets. Liam's eyes searching hers for a glimmer of warmth when he said to her, "We need a grandmother for our baby." She should have wiped the tears from her children's eyes when they wept for their father.

"I'll be there for my grandchildren," she promised herself,

wiping tears from her own cheeks. "I will be the one to whom they fly."

She carried the baskets into the living room. The floor was still covered with fragments of cupboard. Maggie carried them in armloads to the wood stove. She filled the firebox and, with a bit of paper for starter, lit a match to it. The old wood, dead for hundreds of years, was tinder-dry and caught, flaring brightly in her face before she closed the door. She piled what was left into the kindling box in the corner near the stove. She would burn the rest later.

191

A basket of ashes under each arm, she walked outside and up to the ridge. Before stepping into the woods, she turned towards the channel and Saltspring. It was an idyllic day. A speedboat raced down-channel. She could hear the steady hum of the outboard motor across the dead-calm water. The driver was oblivious to the important event that was about to take place on this little bit of land. She supposed he was unaware even of the island. It was a world apart, a parallel existence. A place where possibilities emerged from impossibilities. Where life could spring from death. Where a human being could begin to grow back a missing arm and learn to live again.

The shadow of an adult eagle fell across her. The great bird soared above her head and down to the water where it plucked out a fish with its talons. Life and death. "That is what it is all about," Alan had said.

She stepped into the forest. At once the light softened and the air cooled. She picked her way over the rough branch-strewn ground. The baskets held shoulder-high to keep them safe, she clambered over downed logs and pushed through tangles of salal. How had she run through here in the dusk without killing herself? "Without killing myself," she said out loud and laughed.

Maggie reached the clearing. The moss was still flattened from the weight of her body two nights past. She sat on Peter's log, carefully avoiding the Indian pipe with her feet. There was no sign he had ever been here with her. Or the children. Maybe it was a dream. Maybe not.

Nestling the sea lettuce basket on the ground at the base of the log, she carried Peter's basket to the centre of the clearing. She knelt in the moss, moisture seeping through her jeans at the knees. Tipping ash into her hand, she scattered it in a long oval. Stretching out in the centre of the ash outline, she felt again the unquestionable acceptance of the earth. Today, not a dying woman but a cog in the continuous cycle of decomposition and creation. She closed her eyes and listened to the forest sounds: the hush of wind through the canopy, two branches scraping one on another, the clear song of a robin.

The grey grief within trickled out of her, filtered from her limbs, from each finger and toe, to sift through the moss into the spaces between the grains of soil. The haze lifted from her temple, the heaviness fell away from her heart, the lump in her gut dissolved. She couldn't tell where she ended and the ground began. Her skin cells had merged with the cells of the plants and soil below her. Incredible.

When she stood, the oval of ash had vanished. Peter was already gone, the fine dust indistinguishable from the forest floor. She had granted his one last wish. Here in an old forest, with big trees, near the ocean. A forest heavy with centuries of decay and regeneration. Peter was now part of this. At last he would discover how a flower grows, how a seed becomes the mighty fir. Fingers of fungal mycelia shooting through the soil, seeking nourishment for itself, and the roots of the giants would draw up Peter's energy and he, part of him, would become the tree.

She touched the rough bark of the closest fir. The ground at the base of the tree was littered with feathers, scattered black and white among the needle litter. She tilted back her head. This was the eagle tree. Maggie reached her arms around the massive trunk. It would take three people, arms linked, to encircle its breadth. Perhaps Liam and Joy and she would come here together one day. She laid her ear against the thick bark and listened for the pulsing of the veins, the phloem and the xylem, the coursing of water and nutrients and that little bit of Peter on their way up to the nest and the light.

She dropped her arms and turned toward the cove where the glint of sun on water beckoned. A hermit thrush trilled its lyrical song. Picking up her basket, she sunk an eagle tail feather like a flag into the mound of ash, then picked her way through a cluster of pink fairyslipper towards the beach and the dock. Behind her, Peter's basket had already begun to decompose.

Maggie rowed northwest up the cove, assisted by the incoming current, the basket secure under the seat. Bits of loose seaweed and wood drifted alongside. On shore, a mink ran across the beach and up the rocky slope into the forest, weaving through the web of roots embedded in the bank. Stowing the oars, she picked up the basket and stood in the stern. The height of tide concealed the umbilical cord of mud and eelgrass between the two islands. Today, Baby Island appeared independent. Free, self-contained, complete.

She raised the basket like an offering and imagined Angel in Peter's arms, together at last. In one fluid motion, she threw the ash into the air. For an instant it hung as a cloud, suspended over the water. An unexpected breeze carried it upward, spiralling, a vortex of dust against intense blue sky. It reminded Maggie of the translucent vapour rising from the down of Angel's head. But it didn't disappear, nor fall to the sea. The swirl of ash darkened and thickened and twisted out above the cove, filling the sky. Maggie, confused, followed the charcoal stain with her eyes. The basket fell from her hands into the water and floated along with the other tidal debris before sinking from sight. But her attention was fixed on the coarse black cloud of smoke billowing from the crown of the island.

Alan heard the deliberate blast of the volunteer fire department siren and his phone ring at the same time. The phone call was brief, but long enough to drain the colour from his sun-weathered face. He paused to pull on his heavy boots before he was out the door. On the kitchen table lay a half-finished sandstone carving of a harbour seal pup . . . its umbilical cord trailing along its belly.

During evening practices, the volunteers often talked about the possibility of fire on the small islands within their jurisdiction. Most of the inhabited islands had no water supply, except for a barrel or two of roof run-off. A few, like the Coopers' place, had a generator and a waterline from Galiano, so water wasn't the issue. It was the time. A fire, especially in the dry summer months, could escalate in ten or fifteen minutes to the point of no return. One evening, they had done a practise run over to the Coopers'. It had taken a good hour to get a crew down to the cove, into a boat and up to the house. That didn't account for hooking up the water. Nobody, including Alan, had any illusion about what they might find as they piled out of the boat and ran up the trail.

Alan was the first of the crew to reach the height of the island. He covered his face with his bandanna to protect his throat from the dense acrid smoke that filled the air. His eyes stung. He could hear the other men yelling instructions to one another as they pulled the fire hose from the generator shed and connected the fittings that joined the hose to the waterline. They all knew it was useless. The others stood by, helpless.

The cedar shake roof collapsed inwards. Flames flashed across the visible pitch of the roof. The entire structure was ablaze. The intense pressure of the heat had shattered many of the windows. The three sentinel trees were burning too; a large branch crashed to the deck as he watched. The roar of the fire in his ears was immense.

He started down the staircase to the deck to see if he could get anywhere near the bedroom, to Maggie, but it was already too hot and he threw his hands up to shield his face. Two of the other men yelled and pulled him back from the relentless heat. It was futile. No one could get in there now. If she was inside, Maggie would never survive. He crouched to his knees; his stomach heaved. Was she in there? He shook his head to drive away his next thought. She couldn't have done this. When she left him yesterday, he sensed the shawl of grief had begun to slip from her shoulders. He thought she was going to be fine. He thought . . .

He raised his head. The wall of flame was devouring a work of art. Now it was a funeral pyre, a cremation furnace. Tomorrow the house would be gone, a black, charred scar on the cliffside. In a year or two there would be no trace of it, the land reclaimed by forest and meadow. Could she have done this? He stood and paced the perimeter of the bearable heat. Trying to conjure up a way out of this unbearable situation.

An explosion blasted from the back wall of the blazing

building; heavy chunks of metal rocketed out of the inferno and into the dry forest. A collective yell rose from the crew and everyone backed away to the top of the hill.

"Propane tank," someone yelled.

Four of the men directed the powerful jet of the fire hose toward the trees behind the house, trying to halt the spread of the fire. Alan threw down his helmet, turned and walked from the scene he could no longer stand to watch.

He found her twenty minutes later, at the bottom of the meadow, above the last vertical fall of sun-bleached cliff. Below, bull kelp fronds swayed in the foamy waves that licked the shoreline. She was spread-eagled in the sun on a carpet of wildflowers. He paused at the top, trying to read the emotions that hovered around her body like dragon-flies. He didn't know what he expected—anguish, hopelessness, shock? He sensed none of these.

He climbed down the steps of meadow, careful not to tread on the tiny blue-eyed Mary, the pale fingers of fringe cup and the mat of sea blush, their compact heads a deep pink. He crouched on the terrace above her and settled against a rock. Yellow monkey flowers poked up through the fine crevices at his feet.

Her hair flared like a crown across the fresh green of the spring grasses. Colour filled her face. She was laughing. Not the laugh of a crazed woman, not one strained by despair and confusion. It was the kind of laughter brought about by a good joke. Her whole body shook with it. The hillside rang with it. Soon he was laughing too, not knowing why he was laughing, her house consumed by flames, crumbling to ash not a hundred metres away. He laughed because she was laughing, and because he was happy she was alive to laugh. She heard him and looked up, her eyes streaming with tears. She waved her arm in the direction of the burning house and yelled out to sky and sea, "Peter! That damned Peter. He finally got his way."

Epilogue
TWO YEARS LATER

Today, I step from forest to beach and the earth stops turning. Momentarily. Time interrupted.

A great blue heron standing motionless on one leg in the tidal shallows, intent on piercing a fish, turns his graceful, feathered head to stare me in the eye. The resident mink, in the midst of cleaning the flesh from an ill-fated butter clam, does not scurry away along the beige benches of sandstone at the sight of me. A belted kingfisher, swooping from the branch of a maple tree, freezes, wings arched, her *chk chk chk* cut short, as I place my bare foot on the sand. The spout of a retreating horse clam hangs suspended above the sand. Waves spilling row upon row across the beach are frozen into pyramids of white froth. Across the cove, the island, now a nature preserve, watches alone, the house a memory held within a thousand wildflowers.

All nature holds its breath around me. I pause too; my shoes dangle from my left hand, my right brushes my hair from my eyes. I sense forgiveness around me, in the quiet attention of the animals, the sea, the trees, the air itself.

The water in the middle of the cove shifts and ripples. The souls of the dead, like clouds of mist, rise from the depths of the sea, where I had put them, bow once in greeting and vanish. The earth resumes its infinite rotation.

The heron turns its attention back to its fishing. The mink grabs the clam and scurries across the rock and safely into the woods. The kingfisher resumes its noisy chatter, diving steeply to the water, and the silvery waterspout of the horse clam plops exhausted to the sand. The waves spill onto the beach. The cold fingers of salt water shush onto the narrow ribbon of sand where I stand. The wind once more works at my hair.

In my chest is the familiar ache, heavy and round like a stone that I feel whenever I come to this place. But I no longer have the overwhelming urge to turn and run, screaming, from the beach. Instead, I walk to the water's edge and kneel. The chill of the sea bubbles around my legs. I know this burden of stone in my chest is the price of familiarity, the cost of history, the worth of belonging to a place. I have been away, and I have returned. I have tried to forget but I could not escape the memories that are held here: the pale lips of a newborn, the smell of Peter as we made love, rebirth by the heat of a fire.

The Vancouver house is sold. I can see my new home at the far end of the cove. A cabin perched at the edge of the beach. Each morning from this day on, I will wake to the caw of the gulls and see the sun on the water. My friends and I will walk through the winter storms and gather herbs in the woods. I will paddle these shores with my lover and play with my children's children on the sand. We will gather sea kelp and shells and I will teach them to weave.

I understand Peter's sorrow as I watch the island shed itself of human scent. The tractor and the dock are gone.

The island will remain forever wild. The fire and I made sure of that. Only the eagles claim it as their own.

And I? I am a part of everything around me, no less than a heron or a clam. The spirits will not let me go. I scoop up a handful of seawater and throw it into the air. Lifting my face to the sky, I feel the silver droplets on my cheeks and commit myself to life.

"Hello, my loves, I'm home."

201

ACKNOWLEDGEMENTS

While Maggie's story brewed in my head for almost a decade and then fell out whole onto the page, the creation of this book is the result of the efforts of many people. In particular I thank the members of my writing group—Lesley Pechter, Denise de Montreuil, Susan Geddes and Heather Martin—for their unwavering support and invaluable criticism. Others who read early drafts and offered helpful suggestions and to whom I am eternally grateful include Tory Stevens, Barbara Moore, Jane Waters, Lynne Moorehouse, Linda Nichol, Robert Laing and Ed Pechter. Anne Boquist from Orveas Kelp Baskets kindly taught me the magical art of weaving with seaweed. OceanGirl™ and Jocelynn and Cathy Johannesson of Krazy Kelpworks added valuable details. My appreciation to Mary de la Valette for permission to reprint her poem, "Sacred Circle." For the wonderful chapter illustrations, I hug my dear friend Lesley Pechter. Flowers for Sharon Caseburg, my editor at Turnstone Press, for her insight, infinite patience and ability to illuminate the truck-sized holes in the manuscript without bowling me over. And to my children, Noah and Camas, I thank you for graciously sharing me with my distraction for so many years.

Ann Eriksson was born in Saskatchewan and raised in all of the Canadian prairie provinces. Ann has lived, worked and studied in New Zealand, in Europe, and all over Canada, from Halifax to the Yukon. She now lives and writes in Victoria, British Columbia, where she also works as a freelance biologist. *Decomposing Maggie* is her first novel.